THE ENFORCER'S GAMBLE

TIMBERWOLF LODGE
BOOK 2

VIVIAN AREND

The Enforcer's Gamble
Copyright © 2022 by Arend Publishing Inc.
ISBN ebook: 978-1-990674-64-8
ISBN print: 978-1-990674-65-5
Edited by Angie Ramey
Cover Design © Croco Designs
Proofed by: Manuela Velasco & Linda Levy

Northern Lights Shifters

Wolf Signs

Wolf Flight

Wolf Games

Wolf Tracks

Wolf Line

Wolf Nip

Copper King

Laird Wolf

Black Gold

Silver Mine

Diamond Dust

Moon Shine

A Lady's Heart

Wild Prince

Borealis Bears

The Bear's Chosen Mate

The Bear's Fated Mate

The Bear's Forever Mate

A full list of Vivian's print titles is available on her website

www.vivianarend.com

PRAISE FOR VIVIAN AREND

"Vivian Arend does a wonderful job of building the atmosphere and the other characters in this story so that readers will be sucked into the world and looking forward to the rest of the books in the series."
~ *Library Journal*

"Steamy and sweet complete with a whole host of colourful side characters and enough sub-plots to get your teeth into. A fab read!"
~ *Scorching Book Reviews*

"There's a real chemistry between the characters, laced with humor and snappy dialogue and no shortage of steamy sex scenes to keep things lively. The result is an entertaining, spicy romance."
~ *Publishers Weekly*

I have honestly waited AGES for Vivian to return to her world of shifters and this new trilogy is just what the Romance Witch doctor ordered! The setting is beautiful, the characters are hilarious, and the best friends-to-lovers story never gets old...
~ *Romance Witch Reviews*

Arend offers constant action and thrills, and her characters are so captivating and nuanced that readers will have a hard time guessing who the villains really are.
~ *RT Book Reviews*

1
___

*D*amn libido.

Stacy Moraine stared glumly across the grassy lawn to where her three boys were—well, *cavorting* was the only proper word.

There was leaping and jumping, all of it mixed with excitement to an over-the-top, puppy-zoomies level. At ten, six, and five, the boys as puppies with zoomies was the perfect comparison.

Which was wonderful. Seriously wonderful. The trio happily at play on the grassy lawn of Timberwolf Lodge was everything Stacy had hoped for. That they were safe and free to be themselves made her heart pound with joy.

The part that made her head pound was the man being leapt and jumped over. Delaney Vezina. He of the strong biceps and rippling forearms. With neatly trimmed black hair, manicured beard and mustache, and almost too-pretty features on his tanned face, he could have graced the cover of *Royalty Today* or *GQ Magazine*.

Gee, Stacy, isn't it terrible that the man is not only

gorgeous but kind enough to spend time with your children? So rude of him.

She turned away to deal with the conflicting battle in her gut and came face-to-face with her sister.

"You need to take over all the cooking as soon as possible." Stephanie balanced her hands on her knees and leaned forward, her nose bumping into Stacy's.

"What are you talking about?"

Stephanie pressed a thumb to Stacy's eyelid and pushed it up, peering into the whites of her eyes. "I could have sworn those egg rolls we had at lunch were still good, but the way you're muttering, you must be feverish. Food poisoning can be a dangerous thing."

Good grief. "You are not getting out of doing *some* cooking," Stacy snapped, stepping away from Stephanie's grasp. "And stop touching me."

Her sister snickered. "*She's touching me.* Lordy, Mum and Dad used to hate it when we did that."

The brief shared memory was enough to make Stacy smile. "The boys do it now as well. It really is annoying."

"That's part of their job description. Number five on the list. *Must annoy your mama daily.*" Stephanie caught Stacy's arm and tugged her toward the house. "Since I see the kiddos are still in good hands, come on in. Let's make those final decisions about kitchen renovations, shall we? You've been driving Blue and Jace crazy by ignoring their requests."

It had all been so sudden, Stacy realized. "I'm pretty sure I'm still in shock," she admitted, her feet moving toward the house even as she darted a final glance back at the boys. "Moving across the entire country happened less than a week ago. And while I knew we were going to be preparing Timberwolf Lodge for guests, I thought we had a full year."

It had been the answer to so many problems. Her close friend, Cassidy Rundle, had entered a lottery and shockingly won an eco-lodge in the Jasper, Alberta wilderness. All three of them, Cassidy, Stacy, and Stephanie, were now co-owners of the majestic main building and scattering of cottages.

This was now home.

Discovering the area was also home to a large pack of wolf shifters had been a bonus. They had already known the impossible was possible. Stacy's firstborn son, Colt, had shifted at four months old—a gift from his military father who had been killed while on tour before even knowing Colt was on the way. To say they'd been surprised was...

Well, Stacy was good at suspending disbelief by this stage of her life.

"We do have a year. Only we also have magical help right now, so it will go much faster." Stephanie stopped tugging once they reached the kitchen area of the lodge. "One reluctant cook acquired, as requested, *sirs*. Off to my next assignment."

Adorable smirk firmly in place, Stephanie snapped a salute at the two men in the kitchen, turned on her heel and left the room.

"Hey, reluctant cook. Come show me how tall you are." Jace Carter winked at Stacy as he held out a hand.

He was as good looking as Del, but in a rougher, motorcycle-rider style. Dark brown hair a little longer, a little messier. Jace wore faded blue jeans and a blue flannel shirt. Typical, ordinary workday clothing. It was the sense of power radiating off him that made Stacy approach cautiously.

Not out of fear, mind you. The man—*wolf shifter*—had already proven he was worthy of being treated with utter respect. Alpha of the Jasper wolf pack level respect.

"I need to be taller?" Stacy asked.

"Not at all." The other man in the kitchen was the opposite of Jace. His surfer blond hair was pulled up in a messy ponytail, and today's board shorts and tie-dyed T-shirt were florescent green and orange. Blue Carter tucked his hammer into his work belt then slid a stool toward the cupboards. "We're building to accommodate."

Stacy eyed the stool. "I'm not that short."

"But you have kiddos who are," Blue pointed out cheerfully.

"And these counters need to be replaced, anyway." Jace nudged her closer to the center. "Grab a bowl from the cupboard and pretend to make something."

"Cookies," Blue ordered. "Peanut butter cookies."

Jace paused with his measuring tape out and frowned at his cousin. "She's pretending. She can make anything she wants."

"But I want peanut butter cookies," Blue whimpered. His obviously fake pout was somehow charming, and Stacy stifled a giggle.

She had no idea how he did it, but being around Blue was like taking a deep breath on a summer day. The traces of nervousness that had struck when she'd entered the room vanished.

Stacy made eye contact with Blue as she pretended to stir. "Mixing up the batter now. I wonder if I should put chocolate chips in the peanut butter cookie batter?"

"Never," Blue said.

"Always," Jace offered at the exact same moment before glaring at his cousin. "Stop it with the Omega woo-woo. Go help Stephanie and Cass with the bathroom wallpaper job and stay out of trouble."

Blue winked at Stacy again before wandering toward the second floor. "Oh, ladies. Prepare yourselves for the arrival of the awesomeness that is me."

His call echoed up the stairs.

It was answered by a shout from Cassidy, Stacy's best friend and now co-Alpha of the wolf pack at Jace's side. "Hide the good chocolate."

Beside her, Jace chuckled softly. He tilted his head toward the upstairs. "Cassidy will have her hands full with those two."

The way he spoke her name made it clear he was head over heels with Stacy's bestie, no matter that it had only been a couple weeks.

"Cass can handle them," Stacy assured him.

"You ladies are handling all of us far too easily. And we like it." Jace grinned widely before returning his attention to the measuring tape.

Stacy glanced out the window, her heart skipping another beat as she watched Del with her boys.

Handling Delaney. Now wasn't that a thought? Touching Delaney, tugging his strong body over hers and losing herself in him... What had Jace said? It was *far too easy* to imagine enjoying naked time with Del.

She stared out the window, shocked when his gaze shot up to meet hers. As if he could see her through the mirrored windows. As if he knew what dirty thoughts played through her head.

And when a huge smile stretched across Del's face, Stacy dropped her imaginary bowl and covered her red-hot cheeks with her hands.

~

A BIT of heaven on earth. That's what Timberwolf Lodge was, Del decided. He couldn't help but grin as he turned his gaze on the old lodge building where laughter rang from an upstairs bathroom window.

"Mr. Del, watch me," kiddo number three demanded, the five-year-old tugging on Delaney's T-shirt with one hand as he held the basketball in his other.

"Ace, don't cheat," the oldest of the three boys ordered his youngest brother. "You need to wait your turn."

"Not cheating. I need to go now," Ace insisted, hopping from one foot in a way that made Delaney wonder if showing off his basketball throws or something else needed to happen immediately. Like a trip to the outhouse.

"Mr. Del, can we go to the treehouse?" The middle of the boys, Blaze's shocking red hair stuck up in a tangle like his namesake. "Can I tell you a joke?"

"I want to show—"

"Stop poking him."

Del had been Alpha for a large and rambunctious pack for years, but right now, with the scent of his unapproachable mate lingering all over her children, his nerves were a tad more stretched than usual.

He snapped up a hand. "Stop the ruckus."

They all silenced instantly. Which shocked the hell out of him in some ways until he realized he'd spoken a little too sharply. Used too much...power.

Damn it. That was not the way to make a good impression on them, and by extension, on their mother.

Stacy. The woman who had made every bit of Del stand up and take notice from the first instant. She smelled amazing. She *was* amazing—the fact that she'd punched Del within minutes of meeting him only made him want her more. Strong, powerful.

Perfect.

His fated mate, although he wasn't going to introduce that truth into the picture for a long, long time.

Del dropped to his butt on the grass and took a deep breath. "Sorry, guys. I was wrong to use my scary wolf voice on you."

Blaze fell to his knees in front of Del, a frown folding his face. Ten year-old Colt copied Del's positioning but sat a little farther away as if judging the safest distance. Not too close, not far enough away to be rude.

Ace ignored both his brothers and tugged on Del's arms until he opened them and made room for the boy to settle in his lap.

Del's heart was about to burst from his chest.

Chin lifting, Colt spoke first. Oldest brother bravery shoved to the foreground. "You were Alpha for the pack. That means you're powerful."

"It does. But that doesn't mean I get to be an ass"—he switched words instantly when Blaze's eyes widened—"I mean, jerk by using power when it's not needed. So I want to apologize. It wasn't right."

Ace patted his face. "It's okay. I can tell you're very sorry."

Del chuckled. "I am very sorry. Thank you for not putting me in time-out."

"I don't like time-out." Ace sniffled a little and spoke very quietly. "Once I got time-out because I bit Robby at daycare. He was being mean, but Mama said I had to use my words, not my teeth."

"You have a very wise mama," Del assured him. "Only, teeth are sometimes needed as a wolf."

Colt took a deep breath. "Can you tell us more? About the pack, I mean. And being a wolf?"

"We don't have wolves, Ace and me," Blaze said. "But we're still pack, right?"

"I like being a wolf," Ace nodded. He bared his teeth carefully, as if assessing Del's reaction. "*Grrrr.*"

"You're a very good wolf," Del said to Ace before meeting Blaze and Colt's gazes in turn. "You'll find out more about the pack, and wolves, over time. But yes, you're all part of the pack. Cassidy and Jace are your Alphas. Blue is your Omega, and you have lots of pack mates."

"And you're the Enformer," Ace announced with glee.

"En*forcer*," Colt emphasized before sighing. "I want to learn more about being a wolf, but Mom is worried. Especially after we got stuck in the water."

The memory of it made Del's blood run to ice. Days earlier, Stacy had followed bad directions, and she and the boys had ended up trapped in their minivan in a flooded river. It had been a miracle they'd been saved, thanks to Jace, Del, and Blue working together. Part of why Del was spending time with the kids that day was to make sure they were fully recovered. Until this moment, they hadn't even mentioned the near disaster.

"How are you guys doing after your dip in the river?" Del asked cautiously.

"I had a scary nightmare," Ace announced excitedly. "It rained and rained and then the toilet swallowed me up!"

"Very scary," Del agreed. He glanced at Blaze. "Did you have any nightmares?"

The boy's red hair bounced as he shook his head. "Nope. You were a good helper. And Colt turned into his wolf and snuck into the bed with me and Ace. So that was okay."

"Glad to hear it." Del eyed Colt. "You take good care of your brothers."

Colt shrugged then nodded. "I like being with them. It makes me feel happy inside."

"Probably because your wolf is the kind who needs to be helpful." There was something about the kid that made Del wonder.

"Maybe. That's why I want to learn more. I don't want to upset Mom, but I need to figure it out. Is there some way you can help me, but not scare her?"

Because scaring Stacy was the last thing he wanted, Del dipped his chin firmly. "I think so. Let me talk to Jace and Blue and see what we come up with." He squeezed Ace for a moment then placed him next to this brothers, all in a row, watching him intently. "In the meantime, we need to practice a serious pack activity. You ready?"

Three sets of eyes focused on him. "Yes, sir," they sang in unison.

Del patted his belly, then his chest. "Start here, pull all your power into your heart, then let it rip."

He threw back his head and howled.

Three little boys joined in, squeaky sopranos above his powerful ringing alto. It was pure magic, and inside Del, a key turned. Opened. A place he hadn't even known that he'd had locked away.

Joy. Magic.

Family.

This was what he'd been craving. He'd fought to do right over the years. Being Alpha to the Jasper pack had been a reward in some ways, a punishment in others. But this moment was pure, sweet joy, The acceptance and happiness in the boys' howls—

Del wanted this forever.

He wanted forever with his mate, Stacy. Wanted to have a family with her by his side. He knew what had been missing from his life, and he was going to do whatever it took to make it real.

Which meant he needed to have a serious discussion with his new Alpha, PDQ.

Amusement struck. He was about to get sneaky in a brand new way because *Alpha* no longer meant only his cousin, Jace. Del couldn't wait to pull a fast one and chat with Cassidy, Jace's mate.

Finding a path forward *and* pissing off his cousin? Total win.

2

——————

"Come with me," Cassidy ordered.

Stacy put the head of lettuce she'd been about to chop back on the counter. "If we want supper, I need to get to work soon," she warned.

"We'll have supper on time. I need you and Steph for a high level meeting, though, stat." Cassidy tromped up the stairs without waiting.

Since she'd arrived at Timberwolf Lodge, Stacy had been observing the subtle changes in her friend and sister. Both were still very much the solid and dependable rocks she'd enjoyed close friendships with for years and years. But now there was something...*more*.

Especially in Cassidy, Stacy decided. While her friend had always been strong and determined, she now displayed a level of confidence that went beyond bold. As if Cassidy had tapped into a new source of power within herself.

Still her bestie, though, so Stacy trusted her as Cassidy guided them through a beautiful suite on the west side of the lodge. Two oversized bedrooms, each with a private bathroom, were positioned on either side of a common sitting room that held two couches, two easy chairs, a television, and a small kitchen area with a table big enough for six.

Cassidy pushed open a set of French doors off the living space and guided Stacy onto a veranda.

"Chair on the right is yours."

The chair in question was a loveseat, with puffy floral cushions and an uber-soft pale green blanket draped over the back. The loveseat and two other chairs were arranged under a giant umbrella, creating a shady nook to relax in on this warm early summer day.

The view was spectacular. Tucked on the back side of the house on what Stacy had begun to think of as the "ritzy wing," the suite overlooked Timberwolf Lake and the cottages. The mountains to the west were also visible, and Stacy sank into the soft cushions and curled her legs under her happily. "Gorgeous."

Stephanie sat in chair number two, hands wrapped around a massive mug of tea. She stretched her legs in front of her, feet resting on the solid wooden coffee table. "Isn't it just? Sitting here is a sweet reward after a day's work."

"I still have work to do," Stacy warned again as Cassidy settled in a chair beside her. "And you're making me feel guilty. Do you want some of my cushions?" she asked her friend, already digging behind herself for a pillow.

Her friend's chair was more upright. Black and copper, it was pretty enough, but starkly solid and lacked cushioning.

Cassidy blinked for a moment then grinned. "Nope. Remember, we're the three bears. You're the Mama Bear, who likes things soft. I'm the Papa Bear, who can sleep on a sheet of plywood."

"And I'm the Baby Bear, who is always *juuuuust* right."

Stephanie sipped her tea, eyes shining with amusement. "Remember that in a minute."

Fine. "There's no arguing with you two when you both get rolling." Stacy stared over the quiet yard. Her boys had gone into town with Blue to pick up groceries, and now she had the oddest tickle in her gut. "Not sure what the meeting is about, but I need to say this first. It's such an odd sensation to have the boys away from me and not with one of you. And yet no matter how I try to worry, I can't seem to."

Stephanie put her mug down. "Blue would tell you that's because he's *magic*." She wriggled her fingers in the air, a combination of jazz hands and sprinkling pixie dust.

Cassidy snorted. "Blue is bullshit and charm in far too high a concentration."

"True," Stephanie agreed before turning to Stacy. "We've had a little more time playing the whole "walks with wolves" game. I think it's because of the pack and those bonds they talk about. Not only are the boys, and you, part of the pack, Blue has that special Omega-superpower vitamin thing. No one will mess with the boys when they're with him."

"Or if they're with Jace or me," Cassidy said with a contented grin. "Being Alpha is a kick. Still figuring out exactly what it means, but so far, it's a rush."

"You've always done well being in charge," Stacy pointed out. "Especially when you've *really* been allowed to make decisions, and not pushed into a box of expectations by bosses trying to micromanage you."

Evil Face Cassidy pointed at her. "*Exactly*. When someone knows their job, let them do the job."

Uh-oh. "I stepped into your trap, didn't I?" Stacy asked. "I know that expression," she said as she flicked a finger at

Cassidy's raised brow. "And that one." Another finger at Stephanie, who was clearly gloating. "Don't keep me in suspense."

Her sister shrugged. "Jace wants you to take these rooms."

"*What?*" Stacy was torn between racing through the suite again or covering her head to hide. "This is the best suite in the house. We can rent it for unreasonable amounts of money to the uber-hoity-toity, as you used to call them."

"Number one, we're never going to rent to the uber-hoity-toity. Not here at Timberwolf," Cassidy said calmly. "Jace informed me that these rooms are too big for a couple but perfect for a family. Since you said you wanted to be in the house and not in a cottage, this means you and the boys are tucked away privately. The north bedroom is plenty big enough for a set of triple bunk beds. And you get a big gurl room of your own because you are a mom but also a person."

Her sister laid a hand on her knee. "Before you start complaining, Stace, let me tell you that I've taken another of the best and brightest suites for myself. It's next door to where I'm setting up the spa, so I can work easily and still escape when I want fresh air." Stephanie glanced at Cassidy. "Jace and Blue are big supporters of the rah-rah fresh air club."

"So is Del. Which means leadership is in complete agreement." Cassidy shrugged. "Jace and I decided to take one of the cottages because it makes his wolf happier than the house. If you agree to be reasonable, it will all be settled, and we can continue with final renovations and restoration. Finalize plans for the grand reopening."

It made sense, Stacy supposed. "It's a very beautiful spot, and I would be happy here. So thank you."

"We all deserve to have some comfort and beauty, because we'll also be working hard over the next while." Stephanie pulled a notebook from somewhere. "Blue gave me a timeline of construction completion dates. Jace helped with a list of other tasks required to invite visitors of the wolf variety. And Del has security and other suggestions we need to go over at some point."

The mention of Del made Stacy's tummy flutter. She pushed the butterflies aside. "What are the next key components?"

"Our goal is to be ready for a September long weekend for a small, carefully selected group of past visitors." Cassidy lifted fingers. "Construction and repairs to be completed. Decorating and fun stuff like landscaping. Housekeeping hired because we're not doing that part on our own. Stacy's spa set up enough she can offer a few treats."

"And you, in the kitchen, with the butcher knife." Stephanie rubbed her hands together. "Time to dream, sissy. Basic meals for daily events. Fun special weekends. Maybe that tasting menu you've always wanted to try."

It was like a dream come true. "And help for the kitchen?"

Cassidy nodded firmly. "Jace's cousin Pete. Not as your sous chef, because that would be a disaster with his ego. But he said he can spare a few of the cooks he's trained from his restaurant. Which means they'd know what they're doing but will do what you ask without being pains in the patootie."

"And in terms of the boys, you'll have the best on-site daycare ever," Stephanie promised. "You can see them anytime you like, but they'll also be more entertained than being underfoot in the kitchen."

More than a dream. Stacy shook her head. "How did we get so lucky?"

The question lacked all the details. Like the amazingness of having wolves to be with Colt. A place that was safe for all three of her boys. A place to cook and yet relax, and to be with her friends and...

Her friend leaned forward and met her gaze. "Sometimes good things happen to good people. Maybe that's all it is."

Across from her, Stephanie grimaced for a moment before her sunny smile returned. "You're good people. You and Cass. So yes, there's work to be done. Plus some awkward people to deal with—because there's always people to deal with. But we're together. We can do anything, right?"

Stacy held up her fist and waited for her friends to add theirs to the triangle. "Power triplets, activate."

Her girls both grinned now, big and bright.

"Zippy," Cassidy pronounced.

"Zappity." Steph's eyes flashed.

"*Zoom.*" Stacy completed the ritual as they all tapped the back of their fists together then sat up straight as if ready for battle. She pushed down her doubts and fears and decided to concentrate on enjoying the magic of it all.

There was a lot to learn here at Timberwolf Lodge. Things to learn about wolves and about running a kitchen mostly by herself, *oh my goodness...*

But it was a good new step on the journey. She needed to be sure she didn't get distracted by anything, or *anyone*, along the way.

No matter how much she wanted to.

～

DEL HADN'T HAD a chance to have that discussion yet. The one that would start the wheels turning toward his ultimate goal. He'd barely handed over the boys to a grinning Blue when Jace had commandeered him to help with a project.

"I do have a real job," Del reminded his cousin as he stood on the roof of one of the larger cabins that was tucked closer to the trees.

On the ground below Del, Jace just grinned. He tossed a bundle of shingles to the roof as if it were a pillow. "Good thing you're such an overachiever that you've trained your staff to basically run the law office without you."

"Ass," Del muttered. He turned his back and went to his knees to nail down the first row.

"Hey, that was a compliment." Another bundle landed to Del's left, inches from his hip. "Good to see you still remember how to do manual labour."

"As if I'd have forgotten. Summers were a perfect mix of running wild and being free labour for Uncle Jim out here at the lodge."

Another pack of shingles hit the roof, even closer this time. Del ignored it again. Bastard wanted to get a rise out of him? Nope. Not happening.

A second later, Jace's grinning face appeared at the edge of the roofline. "Slide over and let me get ahead of you. I'll cut and lay out, you nail."

"Of course. Good to let the person with the highest skill set do the more important task."

It was meant to be a cut, but Jace only grinned harder. "Exactly, my good man. Exactly."

Fuck. Del finished nailing down the row before turning on the other man. "What did you do?"

Jace pressed a hand to his chest. "Moi?"

Lifting the hammer in the air, Del eyed the distance between the two of them. "Tempting. So very tempting..."

A sharp laugh rang on the air. "Yeah, *no*. You're not about to beam me with a blunt object. But you are going to be thanking me profusely very soon."

"For being an ass? Thanks, you've really got that one dialed in."

The banter between them was expected. Light and almost playful, it was a way to work out some uneasy edges of power between them.

When Del had become Alpha years ago, he'd done it for many reasons. Never in a million lifetimes would he confess that had included saving Jace from being a hero when he didn't want to be one.

The details of how and why didn't matter right now. The tension of having two extremely powerful Alpha wolves in the same territory—they were still on a rickety teeter-totter.

Jace positioned another shingle then sat back and met Del's gaze straight on. "I have a job for you."

All kidding vanished. So far, Jace had used an Alpha-level command twice, overriding Del's protests and his wolf. The first time had been the day pack power had shifted.

The second was now.

Del stilled. "Yes?"

Potential security issues flooded into his mind. He was the Enforcer, after all. Or maybe there was a legal challenge that had arrived. Del could deal with that efficiently as well.

His Alpha lowered his chin slightly. "Cass and I are very concerned."

Well, hell. Cassidy too? If both halves of his Alpha pair were worried, this was big. Like capital-B Big. "I'll do everything in my power to fix the problem," Del swore.

"I know you will. And Cass and I will help you however we can, but I think it's important to both follow tradition with this issue and be a little forward-thinking."

Del waited as Jace nodded slowly as if gathering his thoughts.

"We have a potential security threat," Jace shared.

He'd known it. Del's spine snapped upright. "To the pack? To you and Cassidy?" His brain raced and the truth struck like a blow. Why hadn't he thought of this earlier? "Fuck. It's Stacy and the boys, isn't it?"

Jace nodded. "Don't beat yourself up over not reading the situation faster. I already did enough of that for the both of us."

Del twisted awkwardly to finish facing Jace. "Is the roof really the best place for this discussion?"

His cousin raised a brow. "Hard to overhear us. No tech. I think so."

This had to be worse than Del had imagined. "Tell me what you know. What's the concern as you see it?"

Jace glanced around the yard. "Colt is an untrained wolf. He's lived for ten years without a pack, which means he needs instruction. Mentoring would usually fall to one of the elders of the pack, but since their family is new and Stacy is here with two human boys, the situation is different."

"I'd planned on going to Cassidy to offer to train Colt," Del confessed.

His cousin snickered. "Well, good for you. She's the one who told me this morning that she wanted Colt trained and you should do it."

None of which was bad. In fact it was exactly what Del would have angled for. Still... "She's one step ahead of me already, isn't she?"

"Good Alphas often are," Jace pointed out. "You did the same when you were in charge.

He had. Which is how Del knew this wasn't the only task. "Tell me the rest."

"Stacy's other boys. Not wolves but knowing about wolves. Heck, they sleep curled up with their brother when he shifts. *Their* father isn't in the picture anymore because, and I quote, Porter Tremblant was *the king of the assholes.*" Jace glared. "That was Cassidy's description. Stephanie was in the room when she said it, and Steph all but turned white at the mere mention of the bastard."

"And now that Stacy is here with the boys, you're wondering if he's going to show up and make trouble."

"It's a very real possibility." Jace cleared his throat. "Someone sent Stacy the wrong directions to the lodge. Directions that nearly got her and the boys killed."

Every neuron in Del's body fired to high. "You think it might be the ex?"

Jace shook his head. "Not sure. Cassidy insists that while Porter took the divorce announcement poorly, he vanished quickly enough. Seemed to find abandoning Stacy and the kids without support was enough punishment."

"He didn't lay a hand on them, did he?" Del found it hard to speak, his words coming out deep and raspy with anger.

"Not according to Cass. Verbal abuse, yes, and emotional. The day Stacy decided enough was enough, things might have escalated, but she'd warned her friends ahead of time and had both Cass and Stephanie there as backup. Porter left like the cowardly bully he was, and Cass said they've never seen him again."

Only there was no proof he was truly out of the picture. A security nightmare in the making.

Del had one final question. "Did Porter know about Colt? That he was a wolf?"

"Unsure."

Which seemed impossible. "This man lived with Stacy and Colt for how many years? Had two kids with Stacy, and never saw Colt shift?"

"Porter left when Stacy was pregnant with Ace. He was only with her and Colt for a year and a half, so while it's hard to imagine, it's still possible." Jace cleared his throat, looking momentarily flustered. "I got all this from Cassidy, which means it's second hand. And she only told me secrets because she had a *feeling* she needed to share."

Big Alpha feelings were not a thing to ignore. "I need to talk directly with Stacy."

Damn it. Having her private information was going to go over like a lead balloon.

Jace grimaced again. "Sorry, but yeah."

Del decided to count the silver linings. "I'll arrange to take charge of Colt's training. And I'll talk my way out of the sharing-out-of-turn problem. But I'll need Blue's help with Colt. The kid's got to have some Omega tricks to have stayed under the radar while just a baby."

"Agreed." Jace held out a hand. "Thanks. I'm glad you're here to take care of these issues."

Del nodded. "Glad to do it. *You* get to deal with the Alpha-level nonsense now, like convincing the old-timers over stale cookies and weak tea that you're not an invading outsider. We're equally punished."

"I'll bring whiskey to sneak into my cup. It's only a punishment if you're not creative enough to make it enjoyable." Jace rolled his eyes. "That last part is what Blue told me this morning."

"Fucking ray of sunshine."

"So much fucking bullshit."

They grinned at each other, both knowing that Blue was, and ever would be, the best of them.

They went back to work, quietly discussing other matters, but Del's brain raced with ideas. Discarding some, analyzing from other angles. Security risks. Training Colt. Keeping Stacy safe. Making a connection with her and the boys. He had so much to accomplish.

Creative enough to make it enjoyable...

When the perfect idea struck, Del nearly fell off the roof. Blue was a bloody genius. Not that Del would tell his cousin that, but still.

He hammered away on his task, grinning as he made plans.

3

———

*B*etween yesterday's measuring and this morning's six a.m. wake-up call, the kitchen had been transformed.

Stacy had seen some of the efforts during last night's dinner. The cupboard doors had been off, and one countertop was missing entirely. She, her boys, and Blue had used the table and one remaining countertop to chop, dice, and otherwise assemble what was needed for a group of five adults and three kids to demolish tacos until they were full to the brim. After the meal, she and the boys had been hustled from the space and sent to begin the switch to their new quarters.

This morning the kitchen looked brand spanking new.

She'd left the three boys still sleeping in the room they'd originally taken—the final move to the new suite was set for later that day once Jace had finished the boys' bunk beds—and made her way downstairs to figure out a menu plan. Not just for today but the rest of the week.

She stopped in the doorway, awed by the sight. Bright

stainless steel counters on either side of triple sinks with an industrial dishwasher a part of the flow. Wooden checkerboard on the counter section she'd use as a baking station. A narrow pantry door to one side of the room, and a wider one to the right. The larger room held shelves upon shelves for dry goods plus an upright side-by-side industrial-sized freezer.

Stacy pivoted slowly. Pale blue paint on the walls, spaces for her to add knickknacks or paintings. A huge fridge, and all the pots and pans and utensils she'd ever dreamed about.

Cooking was both her love language and her comfort zone. Making things for others had been a thrill when she first discovered how expressions changed and hearts lit up, just from the right food offering.

Food wasn't love, but it was one delivery method.

When the possibility of Timberwolf Lodge arose, the idea of being the head cook had thrilled and frightened her. It was a big task, but not out of her wheelhouse. She'd been a short order cook before coming home to be with Colt. Setting her own recipes, making the menus, and dealing with the financial end—a challenge, but doable.

And here's where it all started. Stacy pushed up her sleeves and grinned as she walked toward the massive fridge and opened the door to see what she had to work with this morning.

"Knock, knock." An echo accompanied the voice as knuckles met the wooden frame of the backdoor. "Morning."

Stacy stepped to the door to unlock it. The young woman on the other side of the screen held the hand of a small girl with pigtails neatly poking from either side of her head.

"Hello," Stacy said.

The woman held out her free hand. "Sophie Chevron. And this is Dixie."

Dixie stuck her thumb in her mouth and leaned against her mom's leg.

Sophie scooped Dixie up and cuddled her daughter. "Sorry, she's still tired. I had to wake her to make it on time this morning."

They stood on the doorstep, Stacy examining them, not quite sure what was going on. "Are you looking for a room?"

Sophie's eyes widened, then a smile bloomed. "I'm one of your kitchen help. I bet Pete forgot to tell you I was coming."

Oh my. Stacy backed up quickly and gestured the two of them in. "I'm so sorry. No, I knew someone would be working with me, but no start times were mentioned."

"No time like the present," Sophie offered brightly, guiding Dixie to a chair and lifting her into it. She placed a bag filled with colouring books and toys beside her. "You stay there for now, baby, and play quietly. Mama will get you something to eat in a bit."

Dixie watched Stacy with wide eyes. "Okay."

Stacy hesitated. "Do you want to put her back to sleep? We can find a bed."

"She's an early riser, usually." Sophie ruffled her daughter's hair. "And we were promised that Marvin would be here by seven."

Marvin. Stacy searched her memory for the name. Her sister and Cassidy had said it recently, Stacy was sure of it. *Marvin...*

She laughed when it clicked. "The moose."

"Yes, he's a moose shifter." Sophie took an oversized apron from her purse and wrapped it around her torso.

"When I signed the contract offer with Jace, he told me daycare was included here at Timberwolf. Getting Marvin to care for Dixie, well..." Sophie smoothed the front of her apron and avoided meeting Stacy's gaze. "That was the selling feature to be honest. I mean," she hurried to explain, "working here will be wonderful, I'm sure, but Marvin's the best child-care expert in the region, and Dixie adores him."

"Good to know. My boys can be a handful." Stacy paused. A moose shifter for a nanny. There's a sentence she'd never imagined thinking before. "Well then, let's get some breakfast and coffee ready, because if he'll be here by seven, and knowing how ravenous my three wake up, we'll have a full table within another twenty minutes."

She went and poured a glass of orange juice for Dixie first, tucking the little girl into the coziest corner of the bench seat. Then as Dixie happily spilled crayons on to the tabletop and got to work on a colouring book page, Stacy and Sophie went through the cupboards and chatted about all things food related.

While they talked, the coffee pot was filled and turned on, and bacon and ham slid into cast-iron pans. Sophie took the recipe for biscuits Stacy handed her and tossed ingredients into a bowl without once breaking stride in their conversation.

Stacy found herself listening more than talking, liking this bright, open young woman.

"The pack is great, overall," Sophie assured her after a particularly rich moment of past pack gossip. "I mean, there's always a few people you won't want to hang out with, but we can't like everyone, right?"

"Of course not."

"It's so exciting to have Timberwolf Lodge open again. I've heard so many great stories over the years." She dropped spoonfuls of dough onto a cookie sheet then slid the pan into the hot oven. "Of course, most of that was over by the time I moved here, but still. Jace's Auntie Rachel and Uncle Jim are legends."

"Jace's. And Blue and Del's, yes?" Stacy fought to keep from saying Del's name like a breathless teenager with a crush.

"Yes, and Pete's. And Chloe and Scott and Logan and..." Sophie frowned, washing her hands in the sink. "There are a lot of cousins in the area."

"*Maaaaaaama.*" Ace stood in the kitchen doorway, sleepy eyed and clutching his stuffed dragon.

Stacy took a moment to pick him up and give him a squeeze. "Hey, big guy. Your brothers awake?"

He nodded. "Blaze jumped on the bed, and Colt fell off. But he was—" His mouth snapped shut, sleepiness vanishing as his gaze darted to the strange woman in the kitchen and the little girl in the corner. "—okay. He's okay."

Which meant Colt had still been in his wolf form.

That her littlest boy, not yet six, knew secrets had to be kept, broke a part of Stacy's heart.

They all looked up at the knock on the door. The man outside towered over them, his sandy-coloured beard pulled into a knot below his chin. His hair hung loose around his shoulders like a Viking warrior. He wasn't dirty or unkempt, just very, very big and wild looking.

Sophie turned pink. "Marvin. This is Stacy."

"We've met. Breakfast the morning after you arrived." He dipped his chin politely. "Nice to see you again."

"You, too."

He looked past the adults to the children. To Ace in her arms and Dixie who was on her feet on the bench seat. To Blaze and a now human Colt who'd just arrived, with tousled hair but pristine pyjamas. "There are my targets. Hey, kiddos. Let's get this day started, shall we?" Marvin drifted farther into the kitchen, patting Stacy gently on the shoulder as he passed. "Hang in there, Mama. Things are going to be okay."

Like a hairy Piped Piper, only moments later Marvin had the children settled at the table around him. Stacy and Sophie brought out the fixings for breakfast.

It seemed the first step in a new stage of life had arrived, Stacy mused as the children ate and the rest of her friends and pack leadership slowly drifted into the room.

TIMBERWOLF LODGE HAD ALWAYS BEEN a comfortable place to visit as a child and youth. Stepping into the kitchen now felt different.

Del analyzed and considered as he drank his coffee and chatted with Blue. As he accepted a plate of food from Stacy then exchanged meaningful glances with Jace and Cassidy.

The home hadn't changed. It was *her*, here in this place. Stacy was already becoming the heart of the kitchen.

"Mr. Del." Blaze bounced on his seat excitedly.

"Master Blaze?" he returned.

The little boy leaned up on the table. "What do you call a cold wolf?"

Del considered then shook his head. "No idea."

Blaze's grin flashed bright. "A chili dog!"

Groans and snickers erupted around the table.

"And on that note." Marvin ruffled Blaze's hair. "Okay, kids. Upstairs and into your battle gear. Time to slip this popsicle stand before we lose the whole day."

"Battle gear?" Blaze asked, frowning.

"Code word for not hanging out in our pjs all day." Marvin tapped his mouth. "Plus, we got germs to fight. Gingivitis and plaque are no slouches, so we can't let down our guard."

"Bye, Mama. We're gonna fight Ginger Vitus," Ace told Stacy solemnly before planting a kiss on her.

"You'll defeat him, I know you will," she responded just as seriously.

Colt gave Del a pointed look before following Dixie and his brothers from the room.

"I need Cass outside to make some landscaping decisions," Jace announced.

"Steph, you have to pick locations in your spa room for the plumbing, or I'm not going to be to blame when someone flushes a toilet in a guest room and your spa water goes out of control." Blue tugged her from the room. "I know, I know, your spa will be so Zen no one would notice. But *I'll* notice. I'll be haunted forever by the ghosts of bad plumbing."

"Such a worrywart," Steph muttered. "Fine, fine, but afterward, you have to look at paint chips with me."

The kitchen emptied in two minutes flat, leaving Del, Stacy, and Sophie.

Sophie pointed at the industrial dishwasher and smiled like a gladiator. "I'm going into battle as well."

"I'll help—" Stacy started.

"I need to talk to you first," Del informed her. "Sorry, Sophie."

"Not a problem. I want to figure out the new machine by myself," she admitted, slipping out the instruction book she had hidden in her pocket. "I'm a... I read instructions, okay? And people who don't drive me crazy. So, go. Chat. I'm happy."

What they needed to talk about wasn't about to happen there at the table. Del tilted his head toward the massive front door. "Come on."

He swung the monster portal open wide, the twice as tall and double-wide wooden slab reminiscent of the entrance to a giant's lair.

Walking outside, though, the front porch that ran along the length of the lodge was nothing but cozy. There were multiple seating areas. A porch swing here, a couple of comfortable Adirondack chairs there.

He led Stacy to a set that faced more to the open mountain view than toward each other. Taking off the pressure of face-to-face eye contact might make this easier.

She sat, smoothing her pants over her thighs. Her dark hair was pulled back in a tidy ponytail, long enough to tap the back of her neck. Big brown eyes with a golden tinge. Her lips a smooth curve that held a smile when she was around her boys.

A decidedly *not* smile right now.

He could have stared for a lot longer, but suddenly realized that he was already being borderline creepy. How to do this without frightening her? But without making it too easy for her to brush him off.

"Is something wrong?" she asked before he pulled his head on straight.

"It might be."

Her eyes widened, and Del cringed. He was a lawyer, damn it. He could read a room and draw people the direction he needed them to go. As an Alpha, he could create a whirlpool of trust by simply breathing.

Right now, he had no game.

Impulsively, he caught her hand in his. "Remember right after you arrived? When you said you needed friends?"

She dipped her chin slowly.

"I said I would be one. That's what I want you to remember now. I'm your friend. I want the best for you and for the boys. Okay?"

Another slow head dip. "You're still kind of scaring me."

He squeezed her fingers then forced himself to let go. "Nope. Just assuring you so that you hear what I'm saying in the proper light. Not to scare you, not to mess with you, but because I'm your friend. Can you try to keep that perspective?"

Stacy wiggled back on the seat, opening room between them. "I will strive to maintain a level composure."

"Let's not go too far," he teased. "Just no kicking me until I'm done, okay?"

She snorted. "Okay."

Del went for broke and held up three fingers. "Three things. One easy, one hard, and one just right."

Stacy's eyes widened for a moment before narrowing. "You've been eavesdropping on me, Cass, and Steph?"

His turn to pause. "Umm, no?"

She waved a hand. "The three bears. It's a thing. Never mind and go on."

"One, Colt needs training in wolfish life. He's done amazingly well. All of you have, really, considering. We usually have newer wolves mentor under a more experienced wolf, and I've offered to be his guide."

She swallowed hard. "That's... Well, that's good. He needs it, and I wish I could have given it to him before. Absolutely." Stacy nodded firmly. "Yes, that *was* easy. And thank you. You have so many other responsibilities, and I'm very grateful you're willing to take him on."

"It's my pleasure," he said and meant every word.

Stacy gave him a suspicious head tilt. "Easy, hard, and just right. I'm not going to like door number two, am I?"

He shook his head. "We need to talk about your ex."

4

Despite the warmth rising off the sunlit grass in front of the porch, Stacy shivered. "My ex-husband?"

The skin over Del's square jaw tightened, as if he were gritting his teeth even talking about the other man. "I know this might be difficult for you. Again, remember I'm your friend." He twisted in his chair and met her gaze. His midnight-blue eyes held hers intently. "But I'm also a powerful wolf charged with caring for the pack's safety."

"I understand." She spoke as firmly as she could, but the words came out a whisper. The image of Porter's angry final glare popped to mind, and her skin crawled.

Del's expression twisted, his entire body gone rigid. "Stacy. If I may speak bluntly?"

She nodded.

The man caught her fingers in his. "While I'll be teaching Colt about being a wolf, you need to learn more as well. And right now, you need to know that I'm a male Alpha wolf who senses that you're afraid, and it's just about killing me to not wrap myself around you to protect you."

Someone wanted to protect her from the discomfort of *talking* about the past?

No, not *someone*. Del.

Stacy couldn't explain why she did it, but her gut feeling couldn't be denied. She shot to her feet and took the single step between them to land between his open knees. Twisting, she plopped herself into his lap the same way one of the boys would have.

Heat surrounded her. The strong length of his rock-solid thigh muscles under her butt, the ridges of his chest and torso under her palm as she pressed a hand to his chest, staring into his face.

Rock solid, but once she'd made contact, some element of him softened. There was a slight lessening of the tension at the corners of his eyes. The sharpness of his jawline eased.

His gaze dropped to her mouth and held. "Didn't see that one coming."

For some reason the comment amused her more than it should have. Stacy felt her lips curl into a smile. "I do like being unpredictable."

Del slowed. Took a deep breath then dipped his chin. "Thank you. This is...much better."

She was going to attack him and kiss him senseless if she didn't do something quick. "For me too," she agreed. Then she deliberately broke eye contact and leaned into him, side of her head to his chest, arms curling around his torso as much as possible while he leaned back in the chair. "Is this okay?"

He nodded, and the motion brushed the top of her head, strands of her hair snagging lightly on his beard.

"Is *this* okay?" Del cautiously raised his arms to embrace her, and now she was completely warm and protected, and her heart was doing this weird little skipping beat that made her toes tingle.

Huh. "Yes. I'm...good. I'm safe."

"You are." His voice deep, his breathing far steadier than before. "Can you tell me the story now? Please?"

"About my ex?"

"What you can. For sure about how it ended, and what Porter might know about wolves."

This was so much easier to speak of without meeting his gaze. Not that she expected judgment, but because she judged herself plenty for not being smart enough to have avoided the man.

"I have to start before Porter. My first husband, James Moraine, was in the military. Right before he left on his third tour, I got pregnant. He died as a peacekeeper in a skirmish before I could tell him Colt was on the way."

"And James never told you he was a shifter?"

Stacy shook her head, her cheek brushing the silky softness of his linen shirt. "A loner, maybe? I had no idea he was keeping such a huge secret, not even after three years of marriage. But he was sweet and kind, and I don't really hold it against him. He was a good man, and I loved him."

Knowing would have helped in caring for Colt, but she couldn't turn back time.

"I'm sorry for your loss."

The words should have felt weird to hear, with her sitting in Del's lap and all, but his statement was spoken so honestly, the truth shone out.

She patted his chest under her fingers. "Thank you. But I told you that so you'll understand why I did what I did next. Four years later when Porter showed up and said he'd known James and wanted to spend time with me, it was a connection that made me trust him."

Del's arms didn't tighten, but she sensed him listening very, very hard. "Go on."

There was only one way through this story and that was at full speed. "Porter was kind as well, mostly. He started with visits where we talked about James, and that was amazing. When Porter found out about Colt, he was almost giddy, which was a nice change from the other guys I'd tried to date who all recoiled in horror when they found out I had a three-year-old."

Sadness settled over her like a blanket. Del squeezed her gently.

Stacy shrugged. "I fell for Porter fast. He swept me off my feet, we got married, and a month later, I was pregnant again." It was the point in the story where Stephanie and Cass would always joke about Stacy's fertility, but it didn't seem right to mention that to Del. "By the time I hit three months, Porter wasn't as...nice. He was distracted all the time and having a problem keeping a job. I went back to work, and he stayed home with Colt. When I had pregnancy issues and had to quit three months before Blaze was born, Porter was not impressed."

She paused, wondering what the rumbling sensation was.

A second later, she sat upright, staring at Del's face. "Are you *growling*?"

"Possibly. I'm pissed on your behalf. Ready to go hunt down the bastard and string him up by his nuts." Del said it as if discussing a land title purchase. "Please, go on."

She cupped his cheek. "Not much more to tell. Porter never hit me or the boys, but he began shouting and throwing things. Jumping out from corners as if to deliberately scare us. When I suggested it was time he found a job, he told me I was going back to work, and he'd care for the boys." She made a face. "But he didn't say it that nicely. I was just pregnant with Ace when Stephanie and Cassidy finally convinced me Porter was more of a danger than a partner, and I gave him divorce papers."

Del's eyes sharpened. "He didn't dispute them? Ask for the boys?"

"No. Being involved in their lives didn't interest Porter one bit. He left, and I've never seen or heard from him since. I didn't want child support, didn't want to have anything to do with him ever again. I legally changed our last names back to Moraine as soon as possible." And that was more than enough talking about the bastard, at least in her book. "Now, I need something."

When she lifted her second hand to his other cheek, Del raised a brow. "Warming up cold fingers?"

Stacy shook her head. "Satisfying my curiosity."

She tugged his face closer until her lips touched his.

~

DIDN'T SEE that one coming, either. But hallelujah and hell yeah. Del tempered his desire and kept his hands on her gentle instead of catching her up and taking control.

The rollercoaster of emotions that held Del in a fist swung up into the stratosphere as Stacy kissed him.

He'd been angry, then sad, then hurting along with her at her loss. Furious at her ex-husband's betrayal of the privilege of being in her world.

Now all that was swept away by the new connection between them. This, this moment here, was perfect.

The gentle sweep of her mouth on his. The warmth of her body leaning into him. A steal of tongue over his lips—

Something between a groan and moan rumbled up from

deep inside as Del soaked in the satisfaction of having his mate, his future partner and fated love, delicately exploring his lips.

She'd smelled delicious from the first moment he'd met her, but the taste stealing through him...over-the-top ecstasy like the finest of wines or the best aged scotch. Or a wild romp in bed that would leave them both breathlessly satisfied.

Too much need. Too much want.

Soft and pliable under his hands, Del stroked her forearms and savoured the gentle aroma of her rising arousal.

Far too soon, Stacy eased away, and somehow, miraculously, Del let her go. They sat staring at each other from inches away. Del, because he wasn't about to be a fool and interrupt whatever it was that was going on.

Stacy because she seemed to be searching his soul for some answer to the universe.

"You don't need to stop." Del tried for light-hearted when the silence had stretched between them for a long time.

"I don't want to stop," Stacy confessed, "which is probably a good indicator that I need to."

"Anytime you need your curiosity satisfied, I'm a willing participant," he assured her.

Her lips curled up again. "So I discovered. But this isn't getting to the bottom of your three-things list."

"Life isn't all about checking things off lists."

Stacy pressed a hand to her lips as if in shock. "Oh my. Don't let my sister hear you say that. Such blasphemy."

He was still chuckling when she rose from his lap and returned to her own chair.

Stacy settled and met his gaze firmly. "You okay over there on your own?"

"Maybe. I'll let you know if I get shaky," he promised.

A firm chin dip. "Which means the part I'm going to hate should be nearly over. And you're right. Talking about Porter is one of my least favourite things, but I get why you need to know. Security and all that."

The only reason Del resisted reaching out and tumbling her back into his lap was the scent of sureness now wafting his direction. As if the time he'd held her and the kiss they'd shared had been enough to allow Stacy's confidence to return.

The idea that he could be a rock for her was intoxicating. "Security for the Jasper pack, and because of that, Timberwolf Lodge. But also overall because shifters are mostly a secret. Your first husband was obviously a shifter. Do you think James might have told Porter? Or Porter found out while they were on deployment?"

Stacy considered hard. "I don't know. I have the feeling that James didn't share. I mean, he didn't tell me, and he loved me. Why would he tell some guy he worked with?" She grimaced then wrinkled her nose at Del. "Or am I clutching at straws because James kept it a secret from me?"

This one Del could reassure her on. "No. James sounds like a typical loner. We've seen this before. The type who choose to live outside of packs don't talk about being a shifter, not even to their closest friends. Some of them rarely shift."

A soft sigh escaped her. "Poor James. I'm sorry I didn't know, just so I could have assured him it was okay, you know? That I loved him for him, and nothing, not anything, could have changed that."

"I'm sure James knew." Del couldn't imagine the man

not knowing he'd had a jewel in Stacy. "So Porter knowing James was a coincidence? Coming to woo you was just...because?"

A myriad of emotions danced over her face—surprise, thoughtfulness, concern. "You're wondering if Porter found out about wolves from James, maybe by spying on him, then came to me to find out more?"

"Maybe. Porter might have thought you were a wolf, too."

"And when he didn't find any proof, he lost interest? Got mean?"

The sheer sadness that floated from her hit him like a mallet. Del held up a hand. "You're going to be back in my lap if you keep that up," he warned.

She eyed him. "Um, sorry?"

He shrugged. "It's not your fault. I'm just keyed to be sensitive to what you're feeling."

"Because you're the Enforcer," Stacy stated brightly.

Leaving the connection between them at that felt wrong, but Del let it go for the moment. "To finish—Porter is out of the picture. You don't know for certain if he does or does not know about shifters."

"I kicked him out because of how he was acting and a gut feeling that our relationship would never get any better. Did he know about Colt?" She shrugged. "I suspected, but never confirmed it, and he never said anything. That's the best I can offer."

"And that's more than enough." He'd get the rest of the information he needed about the bastard from Cassidy, then contact some of the packs he knew in the Toronto area. Have them do a little looking around for the troublemaker to be sure he wasn't up to mischief.

Stacy glanced at her watch. "I need to get back to the

kitchen to help Sophie soon. We've dealt with the good and the bad. Last one, Mr. Enforcer, sir? It's supposed to be the fun one."

Time to go for it. It was reckless, and foolish, and way too fast. The words slipped from his mouth anyway.

He flashed one finger. "I'm mentoring Colt." He lifted a second. "I'll keep you safe." A third and final finger joined them. "I want you to date me."

5

After the highs and lows of the past minutes, Stacy could be forgiven for being a touch on the edge. Still, laughing in Del's face probably wasn't the correct response.

She pulled herself together as quickly as she could, but she was still grinning widely as she waved a hand in his direction. "I am *so* sorry. Terribly rude of me. But *what?*"

"I like you. Very much," Del added. "I know this might seem quick, and I know you've just arrived at Timberwolf Lodge and need to settle in and get things running and the rest of it. But I'm being truthful. I would like to date you. For many reasons, and I don't see why we should wait."

"What if I don't want to date? I don't need to date," Stacy pointed out. "I'm kind of busy."

"Do you like me?"

He asked it with such sincerity she couldn't lie. "I don't dislike you."

"You kissed me." He looked her over, a gentle caress of his gaze that set nerve endings tingling. "You look at me, and I can tell you might want to...more than kiss."

Gawd. Still not going to lie. Change the topic, quick. "If that's a wolf thing, stop it," she warned. "Many reasons to date me?"

"I want the pack to know that you're accepted. You need to be seen with leadership in a way that makes it crystal clear that you belong. Dating me works."

She understood what the words meant, but not in the order he presented them. "So a fake date, to make the pack accept me, the human?"

"A real date, with the bonus that wolves see me caring for you."

They were still not on the same conversation plane. Stacy shook her head. "So, what? We'll go on three dates, impress the pack that I'm a good gal, and then if I don't want to continue, you'll give me space?"

His frown deepened. "It would sound creepy if I said no, but...no." Del looked caught between a rock and a hard place. "I wouldn't go directly against your wishes, but I'd change it up and find new ways to entice you to spend time with me."

Um, *ugh?* "Still sounding a touch creepy," she warned.

"Yeah. Sorry, downfall of being mat— male. A shifter male." Del cleared his throat. "Shifters run on a few different rules than humans. We're not a pack that approves of dominating assholes, but...even polite alpha wolves kind of *are* dominating assholes." He scrubbed a hand over his neck. "Fuck. I don't see any way out of this conversation with my balls intact."

She outright laughed again. "You're fine. It appears I do need wolf lessons, same as Colt."

Del nodded. "There's more. But just like I won't drop all the shifter info on Colt in the first lesson, I'm not dropping it all on you."

"Makes sense."

A quick flash of guilt raced over his face, gone the next moment. More secrets? They had to have a million of them, from the world, from each other.

Fine, her problem was here and now. Stacy considered then laid it all on the table. "This is absolutely not why I came to Jasper," she warned. "I do like you. You've proven to be a caring and thoughtful person ever since the first moment I met you. Plus, it's been a long time since I enjoyed any physical connection with a man—since you seem to be able to sense my interest. But interest in sex is not the same as a need for another man in my life full time. I'm a bad bet as a date."

"I'll take the gamble," Del responded instantly.

"And you have to promise that if I ever do tell you to back off, you'll stop. I don't want to have to call in Cassidy to use her magic Alpha-of-the-pack voice to neuter you."

Instead of grimacing, he grinned. "I'm glad you have her, but you'll never need that backup option, I promise."

"Some things are nonnegotiable. We don't lose focus on what's most important," Stacy summed up. "Colt's training. Pack security. Timberwolf Lodge achieving the goal of becoming viable and winning the stakes. You and I are an interlude. Fun as long as it's fun. Over when it's over. Yes?"

His eyes flashed. "Over when it's over. Fine by me."

She could have sworn he muttered the word *never* under his breath.

Stacy took his outstretched hand and shook it solemnly as if they were in a boardroom and not on the porch. Not agreeing to date after kissing and sharing intimate secrets and thoughts for the past hour.

He pulled her to her feet, and she landed tucked close against him.

His voice dropped to the deep and rumbly range that made her skin tingle. "Which means I need to get started planning for our first date. Tomorrow. The first of many. I'll send you a text later with the details." His mouth by her ear, the whisper down to a caress of bass over her neck. "Plus, I look forward to helping you deal with the *physical* needs you've been neglecting. As pack Enforcer and all."

"Safety concern?" she whispered.

"This much pent-up tension could be dangerous," he agreed. His tongue darted against her skin, and something like a mini orgasm lanced through her. "See? But first, time to get back to work for both of us."

She landed in the kitchen moments later, while Del sauntered out the door to his vehicle, a whirl of confusion in her brain and heat glowing low in her belly.

Stephanie pranced into the room, coming to a stop in front of her and examining her with concern. "What truck just ran you over?" her sister asked.

Stacy blinked. "I have a date."

Her sister gaped. "A *what?*"

Shocking Stephanie always felt like a win. Stacy pointed out the window as Del's sporty truck zoomed up the driveway and away from the Lodge. "A date. With Delaney."

She dropped into a chair by the table and grinned.

Welcome to Timberwolf Lodge, she thought, *where the unexpected could knock you off your feet at any moment.*

"And now I need to set something up for us, but I feel like a teenager on my first date." Delaney swung lazily at Jace. "Stop grinning like a banshee. This isn't funny."

"It is from where I'm sitting," Jace told him.

"Hysterical from my point of view, as well," Blue affirmed.

The three of them were outside Timberwolf Lodge, gathered by the firepit. Which meant looking over their shoulders, Delaney could spot Stacy and her boys, clear as day, through the kitchen window. They were at the table making cookies or decorating cakes or something. All sugary smiles and laughing faces, and he wanted to be there with them like he needed his next breath.

He'd managed to stay away for the afternoon and not come back begging like a puppy to be allowed to join in at supper.

But no matter how hard he'd tried to stay in Jasper for the evening, to give Stacy some breathing room, Del's feet had marched him right back to the lodge.

Now Jace held out a long neck beer. "Sit. I can feel the tension in your shoulders from here. This isn't just some random whim you're following, so you may as well stop fighting your wolf and let us help you."

"Wait, what?" Blue sat upright and glared. "We're going to help him?"

"He's leadership," Jace pointed out. "You like helping people. I figured you'd have some good advice for our intrepid Enforcer here."

"After the way he was sniffing after Stephanie?" Blue considered, then shook his head. "No, not so much."

Which was an entirely different ball of trouble. "I already told you I had no idea why Stephanie smelled intriguing. She and Stacy have nearly identical scents. I never hit on her or anything."

A low rumble rose from Blue, and he all but bared his teeth.

So damn annoying. Del waved a hand at Blue and complained to Jace. "How was I supposed to know that he'd sniffed out Steph as his mate? He also hasn't made a single move, not that I can tell."

"True," Jace agreed. "Which I have already pointed out is beyond weird."

Blue leaned back in his chair and put his feet up. "The ways of the wizard are not the ways of the warrior."

So. Much. Bull.

Del kicked Blue's feet off the edge of the firepit en route to the next chair. "Sure, sure, Mr. Omega touchy-feely guru. We both know you were also in the military for a bit, so don't try to feed us that *pacifists feel the ebb and flow of the universe more clearly* nonsense."

"Back to the more important point than us trying to understand the mystery that is Blue—you plan to *date* Stacy?" Jace blinked innocently. "And mentor Colt."

"Yes."

"I see." Jace's lips twitched. "I seem to recall asking you to find out about potential trouble with Stacy's ex, not try to get into her pants."

"I'm not trying to get into..." Del trailed off. He absolutely was, but that wasn't the whole picture.

"Seems as if there's a few questions I also have for our Enforcer," Blue quipped as eagerly as a shih tzu on caffeine. "What are your intentions toward my future mate's sister and her boys? Are you able to keep them in the manner they deserve? Do you have the technology to create the world's first bionic bear?"

Both Jace and Del frowned at each other before turning back to Blue. "What the hell?"

Blue waved a hand. "Sorry, too many late-night retro

TV shows. Steph and I are on a seventies sci-fi kick right now. But the serious question is, are you serious?"

He'd asked it honestly, so Del answered the same way. "Stacy is mine, which means the boys are mine. I've cared for the pack for years, but I've never felt about anyone the way I feel about her and the kids. She's not ready to hear that we're fated mates, not yet." He met Blue's gaze straight on, something telling him this was important. "If you have any ideas to make this work easier, for their sake, please let me know."

Blue's smile bloomed like a rose after rain. "Well, since you put it that, way, magical me does have some advice, starting with what you're doing tomorrow."

Thank God. Del raised his bottle in a salute. "Thanks. After, you can also tell me what the hell I'm going to do about my house in town. Because the odds of me getting to sleep there anytime soon seems to be nil."

Jace offered a sympathetic shrug. "Wolf got you by the throat?"

"The idea of sleeping that far away from her is painful." Del caught himself staring in the window again. He dragged his gaze away only to discover Jace and Blue grinning at him. "Laugh it up, guys, but you realize that until things settle, and Stacy understands enough to accept me as a mate, you're all going to have a houseguest sleeping in the yard."

"Now that we don't have to tear each other's heads off, I'm okay with you being around." Jace's expression tightened. "Wait. You plan to sleep out here?"

"Not about to take over a bedroom and make more work," Del said smoothly, not sure why the comment made Blue break into wild snickering. He leaned closer to his cousin. "What did I miss?"

Because Blue was amused, but Jace wasn't.

Blue grinned and passed over a new bottle. "You'll be sleeping in the garden? Jace won't be able to keep playing his games of naked hide and go seek the wolf with Cass."

Gah. "Please, no. Some things I don't need to witness."

Jace darted an annoyed glare at Blue. "Someday you will decide it's time to woo Stephanie, and I hope you know we will then do everything in our power to make it as embarrassing as possible."

"You'll *try* to make it embarrassing, you mean." Blue pressed a hand to his chest. "Our love will be as pure as the driven snow, and nothing will ever come between—"

"Cass. Steph." Jace called their names loudly enough to warn Blue to shut his trap. "Joining us?"

Blue didn't flinch, just twisted toward them with a welcoming expression as he moved his chair back a few inches. "Ladies. Beer? Mixed drinks?"

"Nothing. Just needed to drop a word with Del, then we have things to do inside." Stephanie pranced up like a sweetness and sparkling light fairy. "Del."

"Steph," he responded, an uneasy sensation in his core.

She leaned in closer. "Stacy says you're taking her on a date."

"I am." Damn it all. He'd been the strongest Alpha in the pack for years, dealt with rebel wolves and unruly visitors without a single qualm.

His knees were all but shaking right now.

Steph leaned in close and lowered her voice. Just a secret between him and her...and everyone else with wolf hearing, which meant, oh, *everyone*. "You hurt her, and I will end you."

Then she straightened and blinked brightly at Jace. She

waggled her fingers at Blue then bounced back toward the house.

Cassidy simply winked. "That goes double for me."

Then the ladies were gone, and Del sat there with Jace and Blue, his pack mates attempting to hold in their cackles of amusement without much success.

Love. Ain't it grand?

6

______

The text message on Stacy's phone had been clear.

Delaney: Meet me at Off The Streets at two. Bring the boys.

Which... Stacy wasn't sure what to make of the sensation fluttering in her belly. It was the date Del had promised, wasn't it?

With the boys?

Somehow both charmed and disappointed, Stacy decided to roll with it.

She arranged with Sophie to finish the final dinner preparations for that evening. They were still feeding only the Timberwolf residents, but maintaining set hours for the staff was important.

And having time off for herself with her boys was also important. Time for things like a family activity in the afternoon, meeting up with Delaney at the local bowling alley.

Stacy shook her head again in amusement as she wrangled her threesome into the cool air of the building.

The young man behind the counter spotted her and perked right up. "You must be Stacy. Welcome. And your boys, of course. Heard all about you." His gaze lingered briefly on Colt then bounced back to Stacy. "Everything is ready. Just need your shoe sizes, and Delaney has your lane all set up."

Carter, according to his name tag, motioned to the right.

Blaze leaned that direction. "Is he here? Where are the bowling balls? Do we pick the pins up after we knock them down?

"Can I have the green shoes?" Ace asked, pointing to the top shelf behind the man. "I like green. What's your favourite colour?"

"I wear a size four," Blaze announced, one shoe in his hand as he presented it to the youth.

Sophie resisted the urge to apologize. Her boys might be energetic and enthusiastic, but they weren't rude. "Children's three, four and eight. And I'm a ladies six." She glanced to the side, but Del was nowhere in sight.

Colt had taken control of Ace, silently guiding his brother to the nearest bench to help remove his shoes. Stacy aimed Blaze there as well, hand on his shoulder. "Questions later, shoes first," she said quietly.

"It smells funny in here." Colt said the words very softly when she joined him, leaning into her side.

"Borrowed shoes might be a bit much for your sensitive sense of smell," Stacy pointed out. "Ignore it the best you can."

"Okay." Colt stretched his neck, almost swiveling like an owl. "I don't see Mr. Del."

"He's here," she assured him, and herself, reaching for the shoes that Carter had brought over. "Thank you. That's very nice of you."

"No prob." Carter examined Colt again, longer this time. "So you're the new...*kid*, eh?"

Colt didn't say anything, just nodded as he helped Ace with his shoes.

Ace had no trouble speaking up. He patted Colt's shoulder. "He's my biggest brother. He's the *best* biggest brother ever. You have funny eyes."

"Ace," Stacy warned sharply, even as she twisted to look closer at Carter. "We don't make comments about other people's personal appearance—" She gasped, then cut off her reaction as quickly as it had begun.

Carter's eyes had gone pure wolf. Big and bright, and even his eyebrows were far too furry to be human.

Stacy glanced around the room, but so far there was no sign of Del or any indication that anyone else in the place had noticed.

So she used her best Mom voice and scolded the young man firmly. "Carter. I don't think that's something you should be doing in public. Stop it right now."

Carter all but jolted on the spot as if jerked back with a rope. His eyes faded to pale blue, and his face de-furrified. His expression landed somewhere between shock and annoyance. "I am so sorry. I didn't mean anything by it."

"Didn't mean anything by what?"

It was Del, standing at the end of the bench. Cool confidence oozed from his every pore as he knelt beside Colt and accepted Ace's hug.

"It was nothing," Stacy said quickly. She offered Carter a warm smile along with the firm mental order not to spill the beans. "Carter was kind enough to bring the shoes over to make setup easier. Thanks again. I appreciate it very much."

"Umm, yeah. Okay. You're welcome." Carter scrambled

to his feet, gaze now darting between Colt, Del, and Stacy as if not sure who was going to turn into the big bad wolf first.

Stacy ignored him, turning her back on the youth and undoing the knot Blaze had been creating in his eager tying attempts. "So, bowling?"

"A nice way to spend time together," Del offered with a slightly pained smile.

For some reason, she was more charmed now than anything. "*Group* date, too."

"That, too." Another overly bright comment as he nimbly caught Ace by the hand and tugged him toward the other side of the bowling alley before the boy could take off sprinting. "Come on, Colt, I'll show you and Ace where our lane is."

"We're coming too," Blaze shouted over his shoulder, squirming as she hurried to finish with his laces. "Don't have fun without us."

Stacy laughed, sudden and sharp amusement filling her belly. "No, you're right. Don't have fun without us," she echoed, smiling as Del winked over his shoulder.

It was not what she'd expected, but somehow, it was just right.

Delaney owed Blue big time.

When his cousin had very earnestly instructed him to take Stacy *and* the kids bowling for a first date, Del had been tempted to hit the man. Now thirty minutes after starting, Del couldn't imagine a better place to be.

Oh, there'd been a few accidents. Like the squished fingers Blaze had from trying to catch the ball Ace dropped.

The spilled pop when Colt backed up too quickly, nudging Blaze into Ace. The occasional lofted ball that had landed with an overly loud *crack* on the wooden boards of the lane.

But the fun the kids were having was golden, and Stacy's expression was pure joy. Del savoured it like a fine wine.

Plus, the WMA gathering in the two lanes next to them couldn't have been more perfectly arranged. Stacy would have to deal with the Wolf Mom Association once the school year ramped up. Here was a safe, non-threatening way to get first introductions over with.

The eight women, all who had children at various stages in the local school system, were bowling and chatting and snacking and drinking with wolfish abandon.

They didn't even pretend not to be studying Stacy and her family. Not only Colt, but the younger boys as well. How Stacy reacted to them, and what's more, how Del did. Fake best behavior simply wouldn't work with this crowd. Del knew it—only the strong survived a WMA analysis.

And he wasn't strong, not at the moment. Not with Stacy wearing jeans that cupped her ass lovingly every time she leaned over to throw.

Like now. Stacy lined up her next shot, standing in the middle of the lane. Her heart-shaped ass right there making him want to jump up and offer to help teach her how to throw, the same way he had with Ace.

"Mr. Del." Blaze tugged on Del's arm. "Can I reuse my favourite ball?"

"Sure, kiddo." Del took a deep breath and tried to focus on Stacy's ball as it rolled down the lane toward its target, but it was futile. He could not stop staring at her body, his mouth watering.

Control, man. Public place. Kids in attendance.

Del snapped his gaze up even as he adjusted position in his seat and hoped like hell the hard-on in his jeans deflated fast enough for him to take his turn without anyone noticing.

From the smirk on Stacy's lips as she sashayed toward him, though, she was all too aware of his struggle.

A long, low *ooooooowww* rang from the left. Del shot to his feet and caught Blaze right before he fell flat on his butt. One hand pressed to his forehead, Blaze blinked angrily as a blue ball with white sparkles spun across the floor away from their bowling lane.

"Grab that one, Colt, would you please?" Stacy ordered. She tugged Blaze's hands away from his forehead, fingers sliding over the goose egg rising there. "Was there a reason you were trying to catch it with your face?"

"Del said I could reuse my favourite. I was watching for it to pop out of the ball thingy, and it did. *Pop.* Then *boom*! That was so cool. Ouch."

Oh damn, this was his fault. Del met Stacy's gaze, but there was nothing there but motherly amusement.

She pressed a kiss to Blaze's bruised forehead. "You'll live. Keep your head *off* the ball rack from now on, understood?"

"Yes, Mom." He tore off after Colt, who handed him the ball with reverence before they assumed positions at the head of their lanes. Feet wide, two hands on the ball. Swing back between their legs, then roll forward and release.

Except it *should* have been a roll. Instead, both kids hefted upward.

Two loud *cracks* sounded as the balls smacked down in unison. Del glanced toward the bowling lane office and wondered if he should offer to pay a damage deposit.

Distraction arrived from their left as the WMA made their move.

"Del. Do you mind if we interrupt for a moment?" Mrs. Holmes slipped between the lanes and smiled sweetly at Stacy. "Formal introductions aren't necessary, but I wanted to say hello sooner than later."

The second woman wore a far more worried expression along with a poofy, glittery scarf. Janine was dressed more for a night at the opera than an afternoon at the bowling alley. "Clara, we should do this later."

Her tone had Del rising to his feet, protective instincts flaring hard. "Problem I need to know about, Janine?"

The woman stepped back slightly, opening space between them as if surprised to see him. "Oh. Del."

Clara rolled her eyes then held out a hand to Stacy. "Ignore her. I always do. I'm Clara Holmes, this is Janine Bancock. Welcome to Jasper."

"Thanks." Stacy shook hands briefly then scooped Ace into her arms when he crawled up on the seat to peer closer at the sparkly scarf around Janine's neck.

Janine kept fidgeting, her gaze darting between Stacy and the boys. "Are you really planning to stay?" she demanded in a tone that didn't border on rude; it moved right in and set up camp.

Del straightened, ready to intervene, but Stacy surprised him by laughing then turning to hand him Ace.

She met Del's gaze firmly then winked where only he could see. "Hang onto this one for me. I have something to deal with."

A happy hiccuping sound escaped Ace as he squeezed Del tight. "My turn to throw. Help me, Mr. Del."

"Mr. Del, my shoe is stuck," said Blaze from the edge of the lane.

Colt knelt on the floor, attempting to wiggle his brother's laces free from the bar they'd lowered to stop the balls from rolling into the gutters. "Stay still, B. I've almost got you."

"Can I still throw?" Ace sniffled as if on the verge of tears. "I don't want to hit Blaze."

There was a battle about to be waged, but Stacy turned him firmly to face the boys. "Go ahead and play with them, please. I've got this."

"Okay." Del caught himself straightening his shoulders as he stepped toward the boys. She had it, she said, so he'd trust her.

The way she was trusting him with her children.

A sense of pride and connection beyond imagining roared to life, and Del focused on untangling three little boys from everything except their growing place in his heart.

7

____

After one final glance at Del to make sure he had it under control, Stacy focused on the problem in front of her.

Which was not sweet Clara Holmes, but the far more tangled expressions on Janine and a couple of the other women in the background.

Stacy had experienced this before. Any new family in town got the third degree. People would have legitimate questions like *Are they good enough for us? Are they going to be an issue?*

She was an old hand at dealing with this...

Well, not the *my son is a wolf shifter in a pack for the first time in his life, and I have no idea what that means* part. Which was a very good reason that she needed to give Del a bit of a poke and get some information flowing, ASAP.

Stacy was even more thankful now for the time spent with Sophie the previous day. The young woman had shared multiple stories about the pack. That would have to be enough ammunition for now.

So Stacy smiled sweetly at Clara then concentrated on

Janine. "I'm very excited to have joined my sister and my friend Cassidy at Timberwolf Lodge. As I'm sure you've heard, we're working to reopen by the fall, which means, yes, I do plan to stay. Both at Timberwolf Lodge and in Jasper. Thank you so much for asking and for the good wishes I'm sure you meant to offer."

Janine opened and closed her mouth like a fish.

Stacy eyed her as if she'd been in the sun for a few days. "Did you have a concern?"

Janine flushed, gaze darting to where Del was bowling with the boys. Clearly he was still listening to the conversation behind him but also enjoying the game. "It's just that..."

She stopped, glancing back at her worried cohorts.

"Go ahead and say it. I won't be offended," Stacy promised. Pissed off, maybe, but not offended.

Janine straightened. "Some of us don't feel our school system is a good place for your children. You should consider homeschooling."

"Janine, what are you talking about?" Clara demanded. "We said nothing of—"

"They're dangerous to the other children," Janine blurted out. "That's what they say. If a wolf goes untrained for too long, they don't have the ability to control themselves." She met Stacy's gaze straight on. "Can you honestly promise that Colt won't hurt another child?"

"No." Stacy answered immediately. Shock rippled through the crowd of women, and Janine's expression brightened the slightest bit, as if she'd scored a point. Then Stacy went for the kill shot. "Can you promise your daughter, Brandy, won't hurt another child? Oh, wait. You can't because she already did. Last year, yes? An incident on the playground at recess?"

Janine looked horrified. "How did you—"

"I'm sure it was an accident, but the truth is, children sometimes make mistakes. Which is why *I'd* never promise Colt, or Blaze, or Ace will not be involved in a childish prank that hurts someone. But I can promise that none of my sons will *deliberately* poke another child with sticks until the poor victim climbs higher on the monkey bars than they're comfortable being, then falls and breaks an arm."

Thankfully, the few complainers were now clearly on the opposite side of the line from Stacy's more numerous supporters in the group. Janine was once again speechless, her expression even more horrified and very, very guilty.

Clara shook her head in Janine's direction then nodded firmly at Stacy. "I'm so sorry about this. We'll deal with her."

"Nothing to apologize for," Stacy insisted. She might not like being under attack, but something felt off. The way Janine and the women beside her looked almost...*relieved* to have been called out was odd. "I don't blame any mother for wanting to protect their children. And Janine is right—Colt's gone untrained. So have I, but we're going to fix that as soon as possible." She gestured behind her. "Del has offered to mentor Colt, so I'm sure—"

"*Del* is mentoring Colt?" Janine squeaked the words.

Clara darted another of those knowing glances between Stacy and Del then smiled. "Well, that clears up so much. We'll just go back to our game. Ladies." She whistled sharply, low and brisk, before herding them back to their own lanes. She peeked over her shoulder. "I'll contact you later this week, Stacy. We'll do coffee."

"I'd love that," Stacy said honestly.

Because while Del was going to be grilled

immediately to nose out any potential future wolf-child issues, Clara would be a far better source of motherly solutions.

One of Janine's trouble pack lingered, the final to leave the area. Patsy spoke softly, as if thinking out loud. "Del is obviously the perfect choice for the job of mentoring. Still, I know you'll be happy once he doesn't have to be around as much."

Stacy eyed the woman. "Why on earth would I not want Del around? The man is delicious."

Patsy's eyes widened.

Making a deliberate word choice for high impact was so much fun. "Was there something else you wanted to share?"

The other woman paused. She darted a glance at Del then turned her back to him. She lowered her voice to a bare brush of air, murmuring, "He's pretty, but he's not safe. Remember that, or you'll end up sorry. Like *him*."

STACY FINISHED her discussion with the WMA right around the time Ace tied his laces to both his brothers' shoes.

Which meant all three boys were settled on the bench by the front entrance, getting their own shoes back on while Delaney worked to untangle the gordian knot the youngest had created.

"Time was up," Colt informed his mom as she joined them. "I got a strike."

"I got a spare," Blaze announced.

Not to be left out, Ace obviously flipped into furious thought mode, a crease between his brows before he announced excitedly, "I got a...sprocket."

"Good for you." Stacy ruffled his hair. "Is our date over, then?"

Not a chance. Not before Del got to have at least a little time with her closer than five feet away.

He shook his head. "I thought we'd enjoy some..." He trailed off and considered. Checking before announcing seemed prudent. "I-c-e c-r-e-a-m. If that's okay with you."

"Yes!" Blaze leapt to his feet and whirled on Ace. "We're going for *ice cream*."

"I scream, you scream, we all scream for ice cream," Blaze and Ace sang as they danced in circles around Colt.

Their older brother grinned widely and then caught their hands and tugged them to a stop by his side. He tilted his face toward Del. "We do like ice cream. It was the first word that Blaze learned to spell."

"So I see." Del started to check with Stacy, but she was returning the shoes to the counter, pausing to speak to the young wolf working the desk. The one whom something had happened with right before Del had arrived.

It seemed outings with Stacy and the boys were going to be highly entertaining.

They headed out the door and down the street to the ice cream parlour. The business had set up for summer, which meant they could order outside and stay outside, which was great because despite the past hour of activity, the boys still seemed to have an endless supply of energy.

By the time they were all settled with cones in hand, Del was ready for a break.

Stacy offered him a pat on the shoulder. "Relax, I'm on watch now."

Del blinked. "Was I not relaxed?"

She shrugged. "Not really. But you're usually watchful when anyone else is around. Even at Timberwolf Lodge, I noticed you stay on high alert. As if you need to be aware of your surroundings all the time."

"Enforcer," he offered as an excuse.

She lifted a brow.

Um. "Carryover from being Alpha?"

Now her expression softened. "Tell me about that."

"What do you want to know?"

Stacy snorted softly. "Everything?"

"That might take longer than three single scoop cones provide," he pointed out.

"Then you should start with the most important parts, and we'll chat again later until we get to the end." She licked her cone firmly, and all thoughts of pack and Alpha and Enforcer fled south along with the blood supplying his brain.

God, his cock was going to kill him.

Del turned away enough to be able to watch the boys and not the way her tongue was working her ice cream cone. "Specific question regarding Alphas?"

"You were the Alpha for Jasper. Now you're not. Does that upset you?"

This line of questioning he could deal with easily. "Jace clearly was the better wolf for the job. My wolf relinquished command willingly, especially after being offered the Enforcer role."

"So there's no lingering bad feelings between you and Jace?"

He chuckled softly. "Holding a grudge because he took my job? That's a human emotion. I was Alpha because I had to be. I did it well until I didn't need to do it anymore. Now I'll be the Enforcer the pack needs, and that satisfies both my human and wolf sides."

Stacy nodded slowly as if filling in charts in her head. "I

need you to tell me a lot more. Especially about being wolves, because Cassidy will tell me what she can, but she's learning as she goes along."

"She's also an Alpha. Not everything she learns will apply to you," he warned.

Another nod. Stacy eased her leg against his. "Will you tell me more later? Like tonight? *After* the boys are in bed?"

His heart was about to pound out of his chest. "I'd like that. I thought maybe..." No, this was his job, damn it. No need to ease around the topic. "After supper I'm going to train Colt. If you want to be there, that's fine. In fact, you should be. Some days I'll have the other boys join us as well, but for tonight, I'd like it to be just Colt. Okay?"

Stacy's expression grew serious. "Absolutely. I'll arrange with Steph to watch Ace and Blaze. Colt and I will be ready when you are."

"And after he's done," Del slid his fingers over her thigh for the briefest moment. "Maybe we can *chat* some more ourselves."

A soft flush coloured her cheeks. "I have a wonderful balcony where we could chat quietly."

"I'd like that." Mischief danced in his belly along with desire. "Good to know you're not afraid of dangerous Delaney."

Stacy lowered her lashes. "You heard that?"

"I heard that and more." He grinned. "Delicious, eh?"

"Hmmm." She caught him off guard and took a slow, deliberate lick of her cone before he could look away.

He was never going to be able to stand up from this bench. Not for the next five hours or until the first snowfall cooled him off. "Mischief-maker."

She smiled. "Good ice cream."

8

$\mathcal{B}$ack at the house, Stacy was as hyped up as her boys. Still, there was enough to distract her until Del arrived again. She shooed her boys up the stairs with strict orders. "Upstairs and into the tub with all of you. I want fresh clothes, brushed teeth, and no sticky fingers."

"We have to brush our teeth before supper?" Blaze sounded scandalized.

"*And* after. How terrible is that?" Stacy agreed. "You can use the new superhero towels I bought when you're clean. I'll bring them up in a few minutes," she told them over loud cheers.

Her sons scampered out of sight, and she sighed happily, turning to discover Cassidy and Jace curled up together on the couch in the living room, watching with amused expressions.

"Sorry for interrupting," she said.

Jace waved a hand. "Not at all. Love seeing you with the boys. You're a good mama."

"The best," Cassidy agreed from where she lounged with her legs draped over Jace's. Their hands were linked in her lap. Their position was intimate, but not embarrassingly so.

"Love seeing you two like this," Stacy shared as well. "You look good together."

"A perfect set," Jace said smoothly, stretching his free arm along the back of the couch, encircling Cassidy within his embrace. "How was the trip to the bowling alley? Other than somehow sticky?"

She was about to answer with off the cuff generic nonsense when she caught a gleam in Cassidy's eyes. Stacy planted her fists on her hips. "You already know about the visit from the WMA."

Cassidy wrinkled her nose. "Wolf gossip travels faster than small-town gossip, which travels faster than seniors-home gossip."

"Speed of light?"

"Tesseract." Cassidy's grin was huge now. "Heard you took care of things just fine."

Stacy waved a hand. "They're just moms worried about their kids. We talked it out. It's all fine."

Both Jace and Cassidy nodded, but Jace's expression tightened. "Just remember that if you ever feel there's a need for more than talking through an issue, we're here. That's our job as Alphas."

"I know. And since that's always been Cassidy's job as my friend, it's not as if this is new territory. Not that part of it," Stacy teased.

"Huh." Cassidy raised a brow and considered. "She's got a point."

"I'll leave you two alone until dinner." Stacy took a couple steps then asked. "Oh, do either of you know where Steph is?"

"Spa rooms. She got a delivery, and Blue is helping her unpack it."

Stacy left the two of them talking quietly, the connection between them like a living, breathing thing. She wasn't exactly jealous, but it was something that was missing in her own life.

She'd loved James, and he'd been good to her, but he'd also been away for months of every year they'd been together. She and Porter had seemed to share a connection until they'd shared nothing but fear and disdain.

What would it be like to have a true soul-deep relationship with someone?

Remembering the caress of Del's whiskers along her jawline made her shiver with desire. Okay, soul-deep would be nice, but a little red-hot passion would be a suitable first step. She missed being touched like she was a treasure. As if bringing her pleasure was important.

Her mind on Del's strong hands and what he'd be like using them was in her brain when she swung open the door to Stephanie's spa. "Hey sis, you have those..."

Boxes with their lids hanging open were scattered on the side counters. The window was up all the way, and a warm summer breeze blew in, making the wind chimes Stephanie had hung tinkle like fairy bells. Louder, though, was a low, rumbling sound that echoed through the room, powerful enough to make Stacy's ears buzz.

Stephanie held a finger to her lips.

Stacy stepped through the doorway then paused, slightly shocked. She mouthed, *What's going on?*

Blue lay on the portable massage table. He was on his stomach with his head turned to one side, still fully clothed. The rumbling was obviously him, but the unexpected part was the pair of pale grey furry ears that stuck up through his messy hair. Fully human, with a blissful smile on his face, and a full set of wolf ears.

Stephanie shrugged. "We were unpacking crystals and talking about some reiki energy flows I wanted to try. Blue offered to let me use him as a guinea pig."

"You need to do more research into the effects of reiki on wolf physiology," Stacy suggested. "He's...blissed out. And the ears are a thing."

"I swear I didn't do anything except stroke his sacral chakra."

Stacy bit back a laugh. "Well, I can see how that might be a problem."

"I didn't know." Stephanie giggled lightly. "He's cute, though."

"Cute, but not going to be able to walk the streets of Jasper except on Halloween eve."

"I can hear you," Blue muttered. "Just too relaxed to care."

Stephanie feathered her hand onto his back. "Um, sorry about the ears."

"What?" Blue reached up and touched his fingertips to one. "Huh. That's cool." He eased himself upright, stretching his neck before peering at his reflection in the window. "Interesting."

"Can you..." Stephanie wiggled her fingers.

Blue grinned. "Sure."

He lifted his hands, wiggled his fingers, and grinned.

Stephanie bopped him on the head. "Behave."

"Or you'll stroke my chakras again?"

She narrowed her gaze. "What happens if I *punch* your chakras? Will you sprout scales and wings?"

"Maybe if I were a dragon shifter." He held up a hand and interrupted her eager question. "I'm kidding. I don't actually know of any dragon shifters, but I live in the hopes of someday meeting one. Give me a second."

He closed his eyes and relaxed his shoulders. A moment later his ears were back to pale white and circular, human once again.

Stephanie looked hugely relieved. "Okay, good. That's good." She patted him again, on his shoulder this time. "I didn't want to have broken you."

"It's fine. You need to learn, and so do I." Blue met Stacy's gaze. "See? We're all taking wolf lessons."

Which reminded her. "Superhero towels, Steph. I have de-stickified boys to rescue from the evil tub."

"On it."

All through the tub cleanup, and then supper, Blue's comment stayed on Stacy's mind. They were all learning. There was no guidebook for how to be a wolf shifter's mom.

But boy oh boy, could she use one right about now.

Upstairs after dinner and cleanup, Cassidy and Stephanie took charge of Ace and Blaze.

"Auntie time," Steph announced. "Ready to be spoiled?"

"Can't spoil a boy. Love only makes him sweeter," Ace recited from memory before bouncing on the spot. "Can I watch a movie?"

"Sure. I'll set you up. Then Blaze, Auntie Steph, and I will go play space pirates in the tree fort without you." Cassidy didn't even blink when Ace jumped on her, begging to be allowed to come too.

"Don't make me watch a movie," he whined. "I'm a pirate. *Arrgh, arrgh, arrgh.*"

Stacy left her youngest two in Stephanie's and Cassidy's capable hands.

Her oldest son sat at the kitchen table waiting for Del to return.

"Need a hug?" Stacy asked.

Colt shook his head. "I'm not scared. Just want to know what I need to do." He wrinkled his nose. "Okay, I'm a little scared."

She settled beside him and held his hand. "Me, too, kiddo. But the truth is, we can't really do it wrong. You know? You're my son. I'm your mom. Those things we do just fine. The rest?" She waved a hand airily. "Details."

He rested his head on her arm. "I love you, Mom."

"Love you too, sweetheart."

DEL HADN'T MEANT to eavesdrop, but the words were shared in the moment before he opened the kitchen door. Clear and pure. Sweet and bright, they drifted on the air through the open screen door and filled his heart with hope.

The sacrificial all-giving love of a mother for her child. The trusting love of a child for their mom. Whatever Del needed to teach Colt faded in significance.

Stacy was right. They already had the most important part down pat.

With that thought in mind, he smiled as he approached the table. "Hey. You ready for this?"

Stomping rang through the living room along with a chorus of pirate-like shouts. Then the big door slammed shut, leaving a stillness behind.

Stacy dipped her chin. "The invaders have left us. We have possession of the entire castle."

"Good, because this isn't really a kitchen table talk," Del informed Colt. "Come on. Let's find a better spot."

They ended up in Stacy's suite. The family room was mostly clear, and that's where Del settled with Colt on the floor beside him, both leaning on the couch at their backs.

Stacy curled up in an easy chair opposite them, wrapping herself in a cozy blanket.

Del twisted away from her, all cozy and enticing, to focus solely on his student.

"First, let's make this clear," Del assured Colt. "You *are* a wolf shifter. Period. You've been one since you were born. Your mom said you shifted when you were about four months old, which is when just about everyone shifts for the first time. You don't need to learn to be a wolf. You need the boring other stuff, okay?"

Relief nearly dripped off the kid. "I'm not doing it wrong?"

Del laughed. "Nope. You *can't* wolf wrong. So let's focus on the other parts. You haven't had a pack, which means you haven't learned etiquette. Which is fancy word for having good manners."

Colt wrinkled his nose, a clear tell he was thinking hard. "Like saying please and thank you?"

"Yup, only the wolf version. Which is still about being polite, but the rules are different because we're not only humans trying to make communication smoother. We're also wolves, so please and thank you sound different."

The boy nodded. "Okay."

Del had done his homework, so the important parts were as simple as possible. *Not everything at once,* he reminded himself. "As well as manners, there are physical tricks we learn from more experienced wolves. You might have figured out some of these on your own, but since you were also living in a city, I'll make sure you get to practice all the things this summer that your classmates already know by the time school rolls around."

Colt's lips twitched. "Maybe you can teach me a few that they won't know yet."

"Smart kid. We'll see how it goes." Del leaned forward and let Colt see him take a long, slow sniff. "Another part of the physical isn't about shifting but using what we have while in human form. For example, I know you took a bath this afternoon. You washed your face and the front of your hair, but you never ducked all the way under the water, did you?"

The *oh shit* look Colt darted his mom's direction said it all. "Um, Blaze and Ace were taking up all the room," he explained.

"Sure. I believe you," Del said, even while shaking his head from side to side.

Another nose-wrinkle. "I don't like putting my head under water in the tub," Colt confessed.

Del hesitated. "Since the river?"

Colt paused as if considering a lie, met his mom's gaze again, then boldly shook his head. "No, since always. I don't mind swimming pools, or the lake, but tubs are icky."

Which still left unanswered questions, but good enough for now.

"Then you need to remember to wash the back of your neck and the back of your hair. Use a face cloth or something. Otherwise wolves will be able to tell." Del tapped the side of his nose. "We have good sniffers."

Colt nodded, eager to change the topic. "Something smelled bad at the bowling alley."

Huh. Del had caught a whiff of something, but the thought of it had vanished under the distracting scent of his mate wandering by in her damn fine jeans.

Damn it. Some Enforcer he was.

He examined Colt closer. "Bad how?"

"Stinky. Like sweet, but not nice ice cream sweet. It smelled like the neighbour's dog when they came back from the lake."

Del glanced at Stacy, asking for clarification.

She frowned. "You mean Buster?"

"Uh-huh." Colt wiggled on the spot. "The bowling alley smelled like that, especially when we were close to the ladies. Some of the balls were stinkier than others, too."

Stacy met Del's gaze. "Buster is a big old shepherd. He had a run in with a skunk at the start of their trip, but by the time he was home, I couldn't smell a thing."

Interesting. Del placed a return trip to the bowling alley on his agenda. "Thanks for that. I'll look into it. But good job of both smelling *and* dealing with it the way a good wolf should."

Colt blinked. "Um. Okay?"

"You sniffed something funny, but you didn't make a huge fuss over it. Not everyone can smell what you do. Can you see why making faces or complaining would show that you've got a better sniffer than most humans?"

Now Colt nodded like a bobblehead. "I didn't tell anyone but Mom. And now you."

"Right, and that's the second part of being a solid-thinking wolf. Because we *do* need to tell the right people the things we learn, especially the bits that aren't ordinary, everyday things."

"How do I know who the right people are?" Colt asked.

"You'll learn who is on *your* list. Your mom is always the right person." Now they were wading into the swampy lands. "Others are almost always right, but wait until your wolf says they are right. And if your wolf ever changes his mind? Well..."

Both Stacy and Colt stared at him. There was a hint of confusion in Colt's expression and fear in Stacy's.

Del sighed. "And your mentor just broke the first rule of teaching."

"What's that?" Colt blinked hard.

"Don't try to explain what you can demonstrate. Just remember your mom is your number one person, and you can tell her anything. Then trust your wolf, okay?"

"Okay."

Delaney lifted a hand and Colt high-fived it.

"Now to more important matters. How good are you at shifting?" Del asked.

The next second, Colt sat in his wolf form, a young, slate-black wolf swallowed up by his sweatshirt and pants.

Del laughed with delight. "So, pretty good. Not as good at remembering that shifting in clothes is a pain in the butt." Del pulled off Colt's sweatshirt and tossed it on the couch. "Give me a second, and we'll practice tracking."

Delaney stripped, then shifted, power sweeping over him like a wave. Pleasurable and perfect, this was who he was.

Wolf and man.

If he'd deliberately stripped right there in front of Stacy, well, his wolf didn't care. His human was smart enough to take advantage of every chance he got to impress his mate and win her to his side.

Playing a little dirty could only help his cause in the end.

9

———————

ow Stacy made it through the next part of the
lesson without bursting into flames, she had
no idea. Spontaneous combustion? Totally a concern when
Del was naked and nearby.

Crikey and holy moly and whoa nelly. The man was
built.

Somehow she had picked up her son's things, and Del's,
and brought them onto the porch when the tracking lesson
moved outside.

Colt buzzed with sheer delight, tail wagging like a
puppy as Del worked them back and forth across the front
yard. Sometimes hiding, sometimes making Colt hide.

All of it done without a single word spoken. Single
human word.

A huge figure appeared around the corner of the house,
walking toward her with an unreadable expression on his
face. Marvin really was one of the biggest men she'd ever
seen, but now that she was getting to know him, it was
tough to be intimidated.

"I see the kid's getting lessons." Marvin leaned his

forearms on the porch railing. "Good. Good. Del's decent at it, I suppose."

"I suppose," Stacy echoed, mostly amused.

"When it's time for the really important shifter lessons, though, you should send him to me." At her hum of surprise, Marvin dipped his head. "Oh, yes. I'm the best of the best, you know."

Stacy wished Del had gone into more depth regarding those etiquette lessons, because this might be a totally rude comment, but she was making it anyway. "Um, but you're a moose. Colt is a wolf."

Marvin waved off the information as irrelevant. "Power is power. Wolves get all tangled up in their pack dynamics and forget to think big picture." He pointed toward the trees. "Ha—good find. Del tried to trick him on that one." Marvin shouted encouragement. "Good job, Colt. That's the way."

It was entertaining and distracting enough having Marvin there that Stacy's libido had a chance to cool down before the lesson finished. Marvin wandered off, Delaney slipped into the trees, and Colt shifted back and grinned hard at her.

"Did you see me when he was up in the tree? I *knew* he was there."

"You were amazing. But now you need to get ready for bed." A pirate song grew closer. "I think your brothers will be ready to tell you about their evening too."

"I'm going to tell them about being really, really still and listening. They can do that, even if they're human." Colt leapt up and hugged her hard. "I had so much fun. And I learned lots."

"I'm glad." She kissed him then pushed him toward the door. "I'll be up to kiss you good night in a bit."

"Okay. Oh," he turned, "Del said he'd be back in a minute and he needs to see you."

He had? So talking as wolves was a thing. "Thank you."

She wasn't sure if she should go inside or wait there, especially when Del's clothes were in a pile on the porch swing. She wasn't sure if she could face another session of naked Del without jumping him.

Strangely, her gut dropped when he walked around the corner of the house fully dressed. "Hey. Didn't keep you too long, I hope," he said.

"No. You were going to come in for a chat, yes?" None of her fearless energy from flirting that afternoon had remained.

His expression folded into disappointment. "Something's come up, Enforcer duties. I can't stay more than a few minutes."

"Oh. Okay." Another wave of disappointment struck, but she pushed it away with a smile. "You were wonderful with Colt."

"He did great. I had a blast." Del gestured to the porch swing, moving his clothes aside. "I'll have to hold off on the lessons for you though. I really am sorry."

"Your job as Enforcer is important. I understand that," she insisted. "Only, I am disappointed. And I don't say that to make you feel guilty, but so you know that I'm looking forward to when we can...talk."

His gaze slipped over her, and heat caressed her skin like a physical stroke. "Me too. Not just the...*talking*, but also to talk. For real." He picked up her hand and slowly linked their fingers together.

A flicker of fire licked through her core.

"I enjoyed the time with you and the boys today. I enjoyed teaching Colt. I want to talk with you and answer your questions." Del took a deep breath and lifted her hand to his mouth, kissing her knuckles lightly. "I want to lay you out on that soft yellow quilt on your bed, strip you down, and worship every inch of your body."

Well, that was clear.

"I'm pretty on board with all of that if circumstances allow. Just you and me and lots of worshipping, of lots of inches..." She grinned. "Did I mention that I didn't look away the entire time you were teaching. Not. One. Minute."

His amusement had a heated tinge to it.

The thoughts in her head were very dirty and very perfect. For some reason, this man made her *need*, but he also made her feel cared for. Even as they sat innocently on the porch swing holding hands.

Thinking dirty thoughts. Planning dirty plans.

Oh well, mostly innocent?

One thing intruded on the perfection. Stacy hesitated then dove in. "I hate to break this moment, but I have to ask. When you told Colt he could always tell me anything—thank you, by the way—what did you mean by that 'you can trust them until you can't' business?"

Delaney sighed. "I'm sorry about that. There's the downfall of me not being a mentor on a regular basis."

Stacy ignored the apology. "You don't need to be perfect, but I do want to know." She hesitated. "You sounded sad when you said it. And you sound sad now. And considering we were just talking about a very not sad thing, this must be a capital-B Big wolf rule."

"Straight up, a wolf should always be able to trust their Alphas and the rest of their leadership team." Del shook his head. "I've learned otherwise."

Fear and confusion struck. "Jace isn't trustworthy?"

Horror skittered across Del's face. "Oh hell, no. I don't mean that at all. Jace is rock solid, and so is Cassidy. Blue is the most perfect magical Omega any pack could want. I'm not talking about them."

She didn't know enough, but she could find out more without burdening Del with it. "Okay. It sounds complicated, but you'll figure out a way to explain eventually."

Del's shoulders relaxed, and she was glad she'd dropped it for now.

Instead, she cupped his face in her hand. "So. Off to do Enforcer-y things?"

"Yeah."

"Maybe I should send you off with a kiss?"

His eyes brightened. "Yeah."

Then he slid his fingers into the back of her hair, angling her mouth to the side as he pressed his lips to hers. Hot, wet, demanding, and exactly what she needed. A fire inside and out, with the small bite of his grip in her hair and the demand of his tongue against hers.

Quivering pleasure inside, a pulsing ache racing over her skin. A kiss—

A *possessing*. Del taking and giving until Stacy was breathless and lightheaded and clutching his lapels like a lifeline.

When he finally pulled back, her lips were swollen from his kiss, her cheeks scratched lightly from his beard, and her lungs sucking for air.

"See you tomorrow," he promised.

He rose, stepped off the deck, then vanished into the trees.

∼

"I HOPE there's a good reason for me to have left Cassidy when there's a cloudless sky," Jace grumbled as they made their way down the back lane toward the bowling alley.

"We'll know in a few minutes." Del had refused to explain. He wanted the test his theory without giving his Alpha advance warning. "If it makes you feel better, I had to leave Stacy, too."

"I can tell," Jace waggled his brows. "Making headway?"

A heavy sigh would be too dramatic, although Del was tempted. "I'm just glad to finally know she's the one."

"Yeah, you spent a lot of time barking up the wrong tree," Jace teased.

Amusement rose, hard and fast, along with bone-deep gratitude. "I'm glad we're family again," Del admitted.

Jace paused. Stopped right there in the middle of the alley and raised a brow. "Are we about to share emotional secrets and do a bunch of bromance building exercises? Because I've got to tell you that while I'm glad I don't need to eviscerate you, I'm not into a kumbaya snuggle-fest."

Del snorted. "No worries, just expressing my gratitude that the screw ups of the past didn't end up messing with our futures forever."

His cousin's expression grew serious. "Me, too. We're in a good place now, and Cassidy would say that's what counts."

He held up his fist and Del tapped their knuckles together. Firmly.

Firmly enough Jace rolled his eyes as he shook out his fingers. "Jackass."

"Always." Del took the lead, gliding noiselessly toward the back of the bowling alley. He stopped beside the dumpster, sniffed, then grimaced. "Rotting food is as good a cover as anything, I suppose."

Jace leaned in close, sniffed, then blinked and turned away in disgust. "Cover for what? Because that stink is beyond obnoxious."

A quick pat of his pockets, and Del pulled out a set of lockpick tools. "We're about to find out."

His cousin watched with admiration as Del got to work opening the back door. "Do I want to know how you learned this skill? I can't imagine it was part of your lawyer classes."

"Blue taught me," Del admitted, standing as the lock opened with a satisfying click. "Follow me."

Del had done a quick poke around the last time he was here, but again, he'd been overly distracted by Stacy's scent and the boys' arrival. Damn it, he swore he could still taste her on the air.

"Remind me later I have questions about fated mates," he whispered at Jace. "This way."

Like silent ghosts, they drifted down the behind-the-scenes side of the bowling alley. The mechanical arms of the pin reset machines stood motionless, strings above, pins below. The ball return curved paths and treadmill-like cups waiting to bring the balls up to the bowling stations.

The strange scent increased. Del twisted to the left and pointed at the source. Jace moved ahead while Del quickly poked his head out and checked the main area of the alley. No one in sight.

A small wooden box sat to the side of three cardboard ones. Jace removed the lid and lifted out a bowling ball. Bright orange with black flecks, it reminded Del of the Tiger ice cream Blaze had ordered.

Jace lifted it to his nose, then shrugged. Only he peered

at the ball closer before snapping his head to the side to meet Del's gaze.

"What the hell?" Jace mouthed the words silently as he took the ball into both hands and twisted.

The two pieces separated. Inside the ball was a mostly empty plastic bag. A faint residual layer of grey powder clung to the inside.

Del's temper flared to white-hot. Drugs. Someone had used the bowling alley to move the same drugs that his father had become addicted to. The ones that messed with wolf metabolism and could slowly drive a shifter mad.

He wanted to rip the place apart. Take every bit of the drug, destroy it utterly, then burn the place to the ground.

What he did was take the ball from Jace, reassemble it, and carefully replace it exactly where it had been. Then he guided a very angry Alpha back out of the building without setting off any of the alarms.

Back in the alley and down a dozen stores, Jace's muttered curses were starting to be repetitive, but Del didn't interrupt. He was still fighting to control *his* wolf.

Protect. Guard. Destroy the enemy. Care for what's mine.

The need to race back to Timberwolf Lodge to ensure Stacy and the boys were okay swamped him. But he was the Enforcer, which meant the entire pack needed him to deal.

He took a deep breath then stepped up to Jace and laid a hand on his shoulder. "*Enough.*"

Power rippled out of Del along with the word. Power enough to make Jace's fury level out in an instant, carrying his Alpha from a nuclear bomb to something more manageable. Like nitroglycerin.

Still dangerous as hell, but not world ending.

Jace's head shot up, shock in his eyes.

Despite the fucked-up situation, Del couldn't hold back.

A soft chuckle escaped, and he patted Jace's shoulder. "Welcome to the wonderful world of wolves, where here and now, I have more authority than you."

"Thank God." Jace's voice was glass shards and pain. "Because I'm about to lose my shit."

"No, you aren't. You're going to pull it together so that we, along with Blue and Cassidy, can figure out a way to catch the bastard who brought that crap into our territory. I don't care if it was a one-time thing. It's not going to become a regular thing. Not on my watch."

Jace straightened, transforming with great effort until he stood upright like the rock-solid leader he was. "That's the same shit that your dad got into, isn't it?" he asked quietly.

Del's heart ached, but he nodded briskly. "Addictive. Enticing to anyone looking for more power." He eyed Jace. "How're you feeling?"

His Alpha considered, then shook his head. "I'm not drawn to it."

It was Del's turn to sigh in relief and say, "Thank God."

"Yeah, well, that says more about how well you've embraced your position as Enforcer than me being some great and all-powerful Alpha," Jace admitted quietly. "My wolf now sees you as a boon, not a threat. Especially now, so again, thanks."

"You're welcome, but we're not out of the mess yet," Del warned.

Jace tilted his head to the tree line beyond the alley, and they slipped through the shadows into the quiet darkness. They ran in human form, still faster than should be possible, until they reached the outskirts of Timberwolf land. Del stopped, and he and Jace dropped to tree stumps to stare up into the night sky.

Considering options. Planning how to remove the entire sordid operation.

"Drugs. I hoped I'd never have to deal with them," Jace admitted.

"Me, too." All things considered, there weren't a lot of happy memories buzzing through his brain right now. "We need to go slowly. Need to find out if this was a one-off or something that's growing. Discover who's in charge, and not just catch the delivery people."

"Agreed." Jace shook his head. "And while this is of vital importance, nothing else can stop. Not the work on Timberwolf Lodge. Not you training Colt. No one should see anything different when they look at us over the coming days."

Which would take some amazing acting chops...except for the part where being with Stacy was the biggest thing Del craved. Spending time with Colt and his brothers was a growing necessity.

Del held out his hand to Jace. "I'll stop at nothing to protect the pack."

"*We'll* protect them," Jace declared. "No one is going to take what we've got from us. Not a moment of joy, not a bit of our connections. To pack."

They shook hands firmly.

Inside, Del's wolf howled. For his pack, for his mate and family.

For the future that was just out of reach.

So close...but not here yet.

10

———

Stacy woke in a tangle of sweaty sheets, cursing under her breath.

Five days. Five freaking days since Delaney had started giving Colt wolf lessons, and she was *this* close to snapping.

Del had lickable chiseled abs. Thunderous thighs of steel. Hellishly delicious granite-like butt cheeks.

Visions of his flawless body flooded in whenever she closed her eyes. His naked skin was all she wanted to feel under her fingers. Night after night the man would lose his clothes, and she'd be trapped there, a willing voyeur to his magnificence.

He'd done it on purpose the first time. Now he was all but taunting her. Even stopping before shifting and giving a lesson while in the nude.

"You need to be comfortable without your clothes on," Del had told Colt. "Humans have issues with nudity. Wolves don't."

Well, *some* humans had issues because *some* wolves pranced around in their unclad perfection and made *some* humans needy as hell.

The spot between her legs pulsed, and she slid her fingers down and cupped herself. Hesitant to continue, wanting release so badly, but knowing it wouldn't be satisfying.

She'd been playing with toys and her fingers for the past four nights, and still she ached.

Especially since they hadn't yet gotten to have that...*talk* time Del had promised. She was trying to be patient, really she was. His role as Enforcer and whatever had taken him away that first night wasn't done yet.

While he didn't make any excuses or share what was going on, she knew. Whispers drifted from the corners of Timberwolf Lodge that sounded like Blue and Del. Conversations between Cassidy and Jace that cut off before Stacy or Stephanie walked into the room.

They weren't so much excluding as protecting them, which made sense. Stacy couldn't fault her friend or the leadership team.

But the other parts that continued? Oh, she could fault Del plenty for that. He trained Colt, shared tidbits about being a proper wolf, then stripped and flaunted himself until she wanted to ride him like a pony.

Two a.m. on the clock by her bed. Stacy sighed, removed her hand from between her legs and tried counting sheep.

One, two, three. Woolen and soft. One white fluffy ball after the other, this one greyer. This one a little sleeker. Not wool now, but fur. The sheep darted over the fence and landed on four paws.

Sheep who turned into wolves? There was a fable about that, wasn't there? The wolf in sheep's clothing, stealing across her floor and into her bed. Wasn't that supposed to be a warning about deception and death?

Something soft slid under her hands. Stacy rolled her fingers and discovered herself stroking cotton batting that turned to fur.

Not a sheep, but a wolf. She was right.

She opened her eyes and stared into the eyes of a wolf. Deep blue, powerful and strong. Familiar after the past days of watching Delaney shift and then preen in front of her.

"Del?"

He nudged her, pushing her back on the mattress. Stacy rolled to her side and stroked him from nose to nape, the smooth bristles of his fur unlike anything she'd caressed before.

Slick, soft. Tingling against her palm.

"You're in my bed." Stacy snickered. "Well, this is disappointing, if I do say so."

The wolf that was Del raised a brow. Didn't matter what form he was in, she recognized the question.

"You planned to lick me all over. It's not happening right now. Not with you in this form. That's all I'm saying..."

He stepped closer. Nudged her onto her back. A blur of colour and motion and he was over her. Delaney with all his perfect *human* muscles and not a single stitch of clothing.

"You humans have hang-ups," he teased.

"You're here." Stacy stroked her palms up his naked back, shivering as the heat of his skin seared hers. "You're really here."

"I could hardly do the necessary licking if I wasn't." Del lifted slightly, his gaze drifting down her body. "Pyjamas are a cruel invention."

"Agreed. Let me..." She wiggled and squirmed, all the while *accidentally* brushing against him. Which meant by the time she was naked, he was hard, and she knew this explicitly because his cock had nudged her belly and her mons a dozen times.

She tossed away the nightie and rewrapped herself around him. Legs around his hips, arms around his torso. "Do not vanish."

"I promise I wouldn't dream of it," he said. "Now, I had another promise to keep..."

His mouth came down on hers, and the magic returned instantly. All the heat, the passion, the need, and the want. Her core pulsed sharply as he nipped her lower lip. A shiver raced over her skin as he scraped his beard over the soft skin on the top of her breasts.

The moment his mouth hit her nipples, Stacy slapped a hand over her mouth and trapped her moan. He sucked, and the pull went from her breast down to her clit, and she was never going to be able to think of sheep again without getting excited.

Del cupped her breasts in both hands, his hips nestled between her thighs. "So pretty. Pale red and soft white. Sorry for messing up this perfect picture."

"Sorry? What are—?"

He sucked again, one side then the other. Nipped at her breasts, pinched with one hand as his mouth tormented the other with exquisite pleasure. She arched toward him, wanting more, wanting...

Minutes later? Years? Del pulled away far enough to offer a wicked grin. "Pinks and red and a touch of whisker-burn. I feel not a bit guilty."

"Never feel guilty. God, more?" she begged.

"Oh course more. I've barely begun," he whispered. "I need to taste you here." He pressed a kiss to the side of her ribs. "And this spot looks particularly sweet."

His tongue painted a long line down her torso before swooping across her belly.

"Del?"

He lapped at her belly button with gentle strokes. "Stace?"

"Don't stop," she whispered. "Please, please don't stop. Give me more, give me you. Give me…"

"*Everything*," he promised. His tongue, hot and needy, opened her folds and found her clit. "Oh, look. Someone was hiding. Good thing I'm a fantastic tracker."

Amusement flooded in. "I'm not sure how to balance thinking of you as a wolf with what you're doing now."

Del kissed her mons. Stroked his fingers through her folds and opened her wider with his shoulders against her knees. He stared down at her sex like a starving dog with a juicy bone.

She really needed to work on her metaphors, because… more dog thoughts?

"I'm myself," Del said, catching her gaze and holding it. He stroked her labia, easing slowly around her clit. "No matter what form, I'm always me. We won't ever do things you aren't comfortable with, but for the rest of it, stop trying to define this. Define us. You and me, we fit."

"We *might* fit if you stop talking and get back to using your tongue for other things," she teased.

"Delighted to oblige."

No rush, just a slow lowering of his mouth over her sex…

Magic rushed in. He had a tongue that did *that*, and *this*, and oh my gawd, *those* things. The coil of need inside her tangled tighter and tighter until she was gasping, fingers tangled in his short hair, clutching tight and holding him to her. Hips pulsing upward, the urge to roll and crawl on top of him so bright that she lifted her legs instead and captured his head between her thighs.

He laughed, the sound vibrating against her pulsing clit. A thick finger slid into her, pulled out. Again, thicker this time. Two fingers? She didn't care what or how but—

"Again. Yes, that. So close, Del. So close."

"Let go," he ordered. Pumping his fingers into her, licking harder.

Pleasure rippled gently at first, like small waves on the shore. Followed immediately by a Tsunami that crashed and pummeled her. Her core tightening around his fingers, tingling fire sweeping through her entire body.

An all-encompassing joyful release that Stacy welcomed with her entire soul. Her legs fell to the bed, her hands stroking his cheeks as he crawled up her body, pressing kisses along the way.

She met his gaze again, smiling at the amusement and heat reflecting back. "That was fun."

"Very fun."

Stacy stretched. The bedsheets moved under her, cool and empty. "Oh."

"What's wrong?" Del pushed a strand of hair off her face.

"I just realized, this is a dream, isn't it?" She gazed at him, wondering at how perfect he seemed. How very real. "I wish you were really here."

"I wish that, too. Someday," he promised. "Someday soon."

Stacy rolled over, stretching her hand over the sheets toward the other side of the bed where she could imagine Del would lay to sleep. She caught his imaginary fingers in hers and held them tight.

Someday very soon, she hoped, as she fell asleep again.

D ɪ ʟ ᴅ ɪ ᴅ ɴ' ᴛ ᴏ ꜰ ᴛ ᴇ ɴ ʜ ᴀ ᴠ ᴇ dirty dreams. Or not ones that he remembered.

Last night, that had all changed. Holy erotic play-by-play.

He stumbled into his law office at eight a.m., wound up and caffeine deprived. He'd still been able to taste Stacy on his tongue this morning, and he wasn't about to kill that flavour, not even with his favourite organic roast.

So he wasn't in the best shape to be acting all lawyerly, but the sooner he took care of matters here, the sooner he could go back out to the lodge to see her again.

Um, go out to the lodge to help take care of important pack business.

Thankfully, his very efficient office manager-slash-law assistant simply lifted a brow when he pretended to march past her on a vital mission. "Morning, boss."

"Morning, Angie." Del pressed a palm to his private office door.

"You might want to slow down a mite," she suggested sweetly.

Drat. He knew that tone. That was her *the list of things we need to discuss is so long we'd better send out for pizza* tone.

Del twisted slowly, rearranging his sheepish expression into a formal, lawyerish one. "Yes?"

She clicked toward him on her impossible heels. She always presented the perfect image for anyone strolling in the door of his law office. Sharply dressed in a red straight skirt and a tailored suit jacket over a crisp white blouse, Angie was polished and exactly what any human would want to see.

Midforties, mind like a steel-trap, and one of the more powerful wolves in the pack. Exactly what the wolves who walked into the office required.

Her power was also a vital point, considering the amount of confidential information flowing around the place.

Angie held out a file folder. "Just a reminder, I have been with you since you first became Alpha. I understand having to juggle your tasks between your law career and your...*other* career. But you need to keep me informed of emergency status, yes?"

Dammit. He'd totally skipped that step. "You knew I wasn't going to check in until today," he began.

She flipped up a hand to stop him. "I'm not your mother to have to listen to your excuses. And I'm not your boss, who gets to dictate your timeframe." Angie looked him over, hard. "But I am your friend. I know you can't always tell me things, and my wolf is okay with that. Just tell me enough to help."

Just like he'd told Colt about knowing when someone was trustworthy, Angie hit every single *yes* button. "I know that, and thanks. How about you catch me up on what's going on in here," he shook the file folder, "and then I'll catch you up on what's happening in here." He tapped his temple.

"Perfect. We need coffee." She spun on her heel and went to grab two cups without waiting for him to agree.

Caffeine was going to help, he decided.

The list of tasks and questions Angie needed him to complete was short. Not surprisingly, since until recently he'd been Alpha. For the past six years, his workload as a lawyer had been more about appearances in the human world than needing a full-time job.

"I've kept on top of the requests from locals for your services. Accepted the few I can deal with by myself, suggested they use the other lawyer in town for the ones I can't." Angie sipped her coffee as he went through the file.

"And how many humans did you traumatize?"

She blinked innocently before sighing. "I did tell one man who wanted to divorce his wife so he could shack up with his side piece that he should reconsider his life choices. But he left here mostly unscathed."

Del could hardly argue with Angie's suggestion. "As long as he didn't see—" he stopped, lifting one of the papers in the air. "What's this?"

Angie leaned forward, obviously relieved at the change of topic. "An email I flagged, considering the subject."

He read it again, grateful for her sharp thinking.

Attention: Delaney Vezina, BA.LL.B
Delivery: general website contact

Re: Stacy Moraine and/or Porter Tremblant

I'm trying to track down a family member I lost contact with six years ago. There was an article in the Toronto paper a few months back regarding a lottery and property in the Jasper area won by a group of women, including Stacy Moraine. I traced your information as the lawyer referenced in the article.

I know it's a possible coincidence, but my brother married a Stacy Moraine.

I understand for reasons of confidentiality you could never simply give me her contact information, but if possible, would you ask if she knows a man by the name of Porter Tremblant. My brother and I had a falling out, and have not spoken for years, but there is now an inheritance to deal with. If Stacy is related, then both of them have the right to a substantial financial gain.

I look forward to your response.
Dwight Tremblant.

Hell. "That's a complication."

"It's also the oldest ploy in the book. Ask for information about someone and suggest there's money involved to grease the wheels." Angie nodded sagely. "Want to tell me the rest of it?"

That gut feeling again hit, and Del shared it all. The lottery, about him and Stacy being mates, the potential dangers, and the local drug issue.

By the time he was done, Angie was mad enough to take apart the bad guys bare-handed.

Smart enough, though, to turn that anger into action. "I'll cover things here at the office until further notice," she informed him even as her fingers flew across her keyboard. "I'll send a generic answer to Dwight to hold him off for a bit."

Del hit *send* on his own computer. "I've got my contacts in Toronto tracking him down. In the meantime, one more request for help."

She looked at him intently.

"Stacy needs to learn more about wolves, and I'm far too distracted right now by...many things." Weak, but true.

She rolled her eyes. "You've got fated mate frustration written all over you. Think I can't see it?"

"Not important," he insisted. "Her learning what she

needs to know is. I'll do what I can, but the rest she needs to hear from a woman."

Angie raised her coffee mug. "I have no problem being a mentor to your lady. Thanks for the vote of confidence." She gave him a twisted smile. "I'll try not to scare her off you for good."

Good grief, what had he done?

11

tacy spent her morning in a happy buzz. Great dream sex would do that for a girl, she decided.

After dropping the boys and Dixie off at the cabin Marvin had turned into a daycare, she and Sophie covered the white board in the back pantry with menu ideas and recipes to try. It turned out Sophie was not only an excellent source of pack information, but she was a born organizer.

"You are hereby in charge of list making." Stacy happily passed over the white board pen before adding a tease. "*I'm* in charge of adding spice to breakfast."

The young woman flushed. "I'll label the spices. I thought that jar was paprika."

"Paprika, cayenne pepper. Same colour," Stacy agreed. "Not a problem. Blue ate all the leftover scrambled eggs from breakfast, and he still added extra salsa. No harm, no foul."

Around ten o'clock there was a knock on the door.

"I'll get it," Sophie said cheerfully, sauntering to the door and pulling it open. "Hell—*oh*. Hi."

Stacy twisted from where she stood with her hands buried in pizza dough to see who had caused Stacy's tone to drop to a thin, worried thread. "Who's there?"

"It's Jessica Gottlied, Mrs. Moraine. Pete sent me to help you in the kitchen." A dark-haired young woman sidestepped Sophie, ignoring her while looking around the kitchen with interest. "Sweet set up."

"Yes, well. Thank you." Stacy hesitated then caught Sophie's eye, which was tough considering she was staring at the floor. "Sophie, take over kneading for me. At least five more minutes."

"Yes, ma'am."

Good grief. Stacy had never heard anything so subservient or mumbled out of the other woman during the entire past week.

And the only change in the room was looking at her with a very smug expression.

"Pete sent you?" Stacy cleaned the dough from her hands, rubbing them over the sink.

"He did. Said you'd need more help than what you already had." Jessica sniffed. "I'm Red Seal trained."

"Good for you." Stacy barely held back from announcing she was Purple Whale trained. She snapped up a finger and pointed at the nearest chair. "Sit," she ordered.

Jessica jumped on the spot, surprise on her face. She hurried toward the table, then faltered. It was if she deliberately slowed her pace before sprawling into the seat.

"Stacy." Soft, so soft Stacy barely heard Sophie speak. "I mean, Mrs. Moraine?"

Good grief. Stacy leaned on the counter next to Sophie but kept an eye and a cold smile trained on Jessica. "You call me Stacy. And we're going to have a talk about a few key things, including standing up for ourselves in a bit. But what did you need to tell me?"

"We do need more help." Sophie's shoulders slumped. "As much as I'd like to say we can do it all, we can't. We can't work seven days a week forever, so we need at least three people to run the kitchen. More once the guests start filling up the lodge."

Stacy patted her on the shoulder. "Yes, dear. I know. I'm glad you know that as well." She leaned in and whispered in the young woman's ears. "But the people who work here will *belong* here, you understand?"

The smirk on Jessica's face slipped. As if she'd heard the whispered comment.

So. Another tidbit of information confirmed. Wolf hearing equaled super hearing. Later Stacy would worry about all the whispered conversations Colt might have heard over the years.

For now, though, she paced over to the table, folded her arms, and stared at Jessica. Didn't speak, just looked.

That look. The *mom* look.

Jessica swallowed hard. Seconds later, she was damn near wiggling in her chair the way Blaze did when Stacy watched him closely after asking if the kid had taken cookies from the cookie jar in the middle of the night.

It took all of forty-five seconds before Jessica broke. "I need this job," she said quietly. "Please don't send me away."

Sighing, Stacy pulled out the chair next to her. "Then why, if you need this job, would you show up here with an attitude and be rude to Sophie?"

"Um, Stacy?" Sophie kept kneading, but she met Stacy's eyes over her shoulder. "I'm a far less dominant wolf than Jessica. She can't really help it. The being rude to me part."

"Bullshit," Stacy snapped before laughing. "You should see your face."

"But it's true. I'm not a very strong wolf."

Stacy pointed at Jessica to stay put then rose to speak directly to Sophie. "Listen to me."

The young woman froze, hands buried in the dough.

Damn. This wolf thing was complicated. "I just meant... Pay attention to this because it's important." When Sophie met her gaze, Stacy nodded sharply. "Good. Now listen up. *You* are a perfect wolf."

"Oka*aaay*..."

She spun toward Jessica. "And *you* are a perfect wolf."

Just like Stacy had told Colt the other day. It seemed it didn't matter how old people got, they still needed a reminder of basic truths.

Jessica nodded. "Um..."

"But both of you are also human. You're women, and you might be sisters or mothers or friends or workers or a multitude of other things. And all those roles have rules just like being a wolf does. You wouldn't march up to someone else's grandmother on the street and hug her, would you? You wouldn't spit in a random stranger's face."

Jessica blinked. "Of course not."

"Then learn the rules that apply here. I am Alpha because I'm responsible for what happens in the Timberwolf Lodge kitchen. Just like Pete is Alpha in his kitchen. You think Jace would ever walk in there and touch Pete's pans?"

Both Jessica and Sophie gasped.

"I thought not. So you *know* it's not all about wolf power. So let's get this straight. I *am* in charge."

"Yes, ma'am," Jessica said softly.

Stacy shook a finger at her. "No. I might be Alpha, but it's *our* kitchen. We all work here, and we all want to make the food that's served the best it can be. Which means other than I'm the one who will deal with any breakdowns or trouble, we work together. Sophie will be good at some things, you'll be good at others, and we'll all be terrible at something, and we'll never, ever attempt to cook that by ourselves."

Jessica twisted her fingers together nervously. "I get to work here?"

"If you can follow the rules, yes. And if being Red Seal trained means you know how to make macaroni and cheese, because that's on the lunch menu and we need enough for..." She turned to Sophie. "What's the number for lunch?"

"Twelve, counting Jessica," Sophie answered instantly, hands already returned to the kneading process. She took a deep breath then looked Jessica in the eye. "I'm good at math and numbers, so if you need help multiplying recipes, ask for help. I know you sometimes had trouble with that at Pete's."

"Um, okay. Yes." Jessica rose to her feet and held out a hand to Stacy. "And yes, I can make mac and cheese. I assume you don't want a version with truffle oil?"

"Not today. We'll save that for a special occasion." Stacy led her to the pantry and pulled out an apron. "Welcome to the kitchen."

"Thanks." Jessica nodded quickly. "I'm... I'm glad to be here."

It was the first thing she'd said that was truly honest.

It was a start.

DEL HAD ARRIVED in time to overhear most of the discussion, and it only made him prouder that this was his future mate. Throwing down and taking names...and quietly using the right amount of pressure to guide what could have been a volatile situation.

Wolves were not always known for their logic. Not when it came to the power hierarchy.

He waited until both the younger women were busy with tasks before catching Stacy's eye and crooking a finger at her.

She flushed as she walked into the living room. "Hey. I thought you were working at your office today."

"Hey. Already put in the morning. My assistant, Angie, kicked me out when I started whining about missing you."

Yup, definitely a flush on her pretty cheeks. What was she thinking about? Hopefully something good.

Stacy crossed to his side then rose on her toes and pressed a quick kiss to his cheek. "I missed you too," she said softly.

They stood there grinning at each other for a moment before he remembered he had one item on his official list, other than ogling her, that needed to be dealt with. "Come here."

Del guided her to the couch, settling with her fingers still in his.

Stacy lifted her chin. "This is cozy, but you have something on your mind."

"I do. Back to our discussion a few days ago, something's come up with a potential question about your ex." Her cheeks lost their colour, and he hurried to reassure her. "It might be nothing, but I need to follow up. Do you know someone named Dwight Tremblant? Did Porter ever mention an estranged brother?"

"Never," she answered immediately. "Porter said he was an only child. In fact," she paused, a crease forming between her eyes as she concentrated. "That was one of the things he told me that connected him so quickly to James. That they were both solo kids who lost their parents early. Dwight must be totally unrelated to Porter."

"Or he's someone trying to pull a fast one. Or Porter lied."

She sniffed. "Entirely possible. The Porter lying part." Stacy shook her head. "So, no. I don't know a Dwight."

"That's all I need right now. Don't worry about it," Del said again. "I'll take care of it."

"That's your job," she affirmed sweetly.

"And your job is to be the Timberwolf Lodge Kitchen Alpha." Del wanted to eat her up in one bite. "You're very sexy when you're all dominant, by the way."

Her cheeks flushed even harder this time. "People hearing every word that's said in a five mile radius is a hard thing to get used to."

"I want to have you go all Alpha on *me* in your kitchen. Want to have your way with me? Order me to make you a sandwich?"

"Is that a new euphemism for *talking*?" Her eyes sparkled. "Not that we've managed to do much, if any, *talking* these past days."

"I know. I'm sorry."

She shushed him sweetly. "Never mind. I'm not really complaining. I understand what you do is important. I'll have to be patient and wait."

"Both traits you suck at?" he teased. They laughed, and he added. "Me too. I want to have more than sweet dreams about you."

She stilled. Went completely motionless. "Dreams?"

Something important had just happened. Del slowed and heeded his wolf's warning. "Did you have something we need to talk about regarding *dreams?*"

She opened and closed her mouth a few times. "Um."

"You have some bad dreams lately? Or some good ones?

Stacy stroked his fingers, avoiding his gaze. Cheeks flaming red. "Is this a wolf thing you need to tell me about? You do know you're very far behind on my lessons."

"I am, but you're trying to change the topic." Del pulled her into his lap and nuzzled his nose against her neck. "You dreaming about me?"

She shivered then nodded.

"I like that. Dirty dreams?" A dream like the one he'd had last night would be good.

"Dirty implies something bad." She lifted her chin and full on beamed at him. "This one was very, very good."

Something he'd heard, once upon a time in a story, slipped into his brain then vanished before he could capture it. He tracked it slowly now, carefully.

Was it possible? "Did I kiss you?" he asked.

"Yes." A soft whisper.

So he did it again. A soft, sweet kiss, barely brushing his mouth over hers.

She smiled, lips still on his. "More of a kiss than that. Firmer. More needy."

"Needy I can do. But did I touch you? Here?" He cupped her breast over her T-shirt, the bud of her nipple curling to a tight peak instantly under his palm.

A soft groan escaped her, and the beat of her heart increased tempo. "With your hands and your mouth…"

"I'd do that here and now, but it might be a little risky, considering where we're sitting," Del warned, reluctantly tugging his hand away.

Stacy met his gaze. "You touched me, and licked me, and I wanted to keep going. You didn't get to enjoy yourself."

"Oh, I enjoyed myself plenty." There was no doubt now. They'd somehow shared the same dream. "Stace, I think…"

"Hey, the house." Blue's happy shout from the porch landing had Stacy and Del scrambling away from each other.

The front door flew open, smacking off the wall behind it.

"Blue, please learn to control your strength." Cassidy stomped down the stairs and glared at him. "That door is going to break the lodge."

"I'm sorry, it's all those beans I've been eating."

Stephanie eyed him with concern as she joined the crowd gathering in the foyer. "You promised to help me work on a mosaic in the massage room this afternoon. I'm not sure I want to do that if there were beans involved in your morning."

He waved a hand. "Not that type of beans."

"Mexican dancing beans?" Jace suggested.

"Magic beanstalk beans?" Stacy had slid to the far side of the foyer to join the conversation. But pretending that she and Del hadn't been all cozied up together only seconds ago?

Not a chance. Jace and Blue offered Del amused grins. They could scent him all over her.

Another thing he needed to warn her about, stat.

But it seemed every time they were together, *being together* was the only thing he could think about. Some Enforcer he was being, led around by his hormones like a wayward youth. He had to stop physically obsessing, at least until the danger was past.

"Tomorrow we're headed up to the hot springs," Jace announced as the group of them, including Marvin and his charges, gathered for lunch. "Blue suggested it, and I think it's a great idea. I've booked the entire place from one to nine p.m., so the whole pack can stop in when it's convenient for some quality time."

"Sweet." Blue nodded at the boys, who were all sitting as close to him as possible. "Swimming in the hot springs is a very good wolf activity," he informed them. "Colt can swim as a wolf, and you two can do the best ever cannonballs."

"Good idea," Del agreed, winking at Ace and Blaze. "Wolves suck at cannonballs."

"We do not," Sophie complained before considering. "Okay, *most* wolves do suck at them."

"It's the random limbs and their tail sticking out," Marvin explained to the boys. "Wolves in fur are like cannonballs with five legs. Not very ball-like at all."

"Hey, Mr. Blue. What do you call a wolf who falls into the washing machine?"

"Oh my goodness," Blue said, hand pressed to his chest as if extremely worried for the poor wolf. "What do you call him?"

Blaze shot to his feet and raised a hand in the air triumphantly. "A wash-and-wear wolf."

The groans were smothered under the hums of delight

at the mac and cheese and tall glasses of iced tea. Del sat, his fingers linked under the table with Stacy's, little Ace on his other side, and he wondered how to make time speed up to get to where this was real, all the time.

Truly his.

12

______

Another nocturnal escapade into a hot, sweaty dream would have been nice, but the only thing Stacy saw that night were the insides of her eyelids. Still, a solid sleep before a big date wasn't a thing to be taken for granted.

Another date with Del...

And all her boys. Once again that happy/disappointed sensation struck.

Blue had driven them to a spot along the road that led to the hot springs, offered Del a wink, then took off.

Del handed each of the boys and Stacy a miniature backpack to wear with their own snacks and water bottles before putting a much bigger pack on his back. "It's a long enough hike to be fun, but short enough we'll all still have energy to swim."

"Makes sense." Stacy retied Ace's laces for the fifteenth time, double knotting them to keep them on. "Don't run off on us, okay? You need to listen to both Del and me today."

"Hiking rules in effect," Del agreed. He lined the boys up like little soldiers then stood before them, legs wide, hands clasped behind his back. "Three rules to keep us and the trail safe. Ready?"

"Ready," they recited back. Stacy's heart gave a jolt when she realized all of them were trying to copy Del's stance the best they could. Colt wasn't bad, but Blaze had his chest puffed out so far he was almost tipping over.

"Stay on the trail, no eating random berries, and keep your snacks away from the wildlife." Del's eyes sparkled as he guided her to a spot at the front of the line then pointed at the clearly marked trail. "Your mom is our pace setter. No one goes faster than her. Everybody got it?"

"I bet you're at the back," Colt said. "For safety."

"Right." Del winked. "I'm the caboose."

"We're a train," Ace announced excitedly. "Choo-choo, Mama."

"Choo-choo," she agreed then headed up the trail with Ace's fingers linked in hers. Happiness swelled inside at the memory-making moment.

She liked that Del didn't expect her to simply make her children vanish as if they were an inconvenience.

Having them cared for daily by Marvin had proven to be a wonderful improvement from the daycare she'd had to rely on as a single mom. Her sister and friend couldn't always be there as babysitters. Although they'd done more than their share over the years.

No, getting to slip out of the kitchen and drop in at Adventure Academy, as the boys had named their school/day care cabin, was perfect and precious. She'd begun to bring them into the kitchen one at a time to help with dinner prep, not so much for their limited assistance, but so they got to be a real part of providing for their family pack. Active and helpful members along with the sweet time conversing one-on-one as they chopped and peeled the best they could.

Time with Del and the boys was somehow exactly what needed to happen today, she thought as she hiked up the cool, shadow-dappled trail. But time alone? As adults?

At some point, she needed to take matters into her own hands. Or more specifically, she was going to take Del in hand and find a way to corner him alone somewhere they couldn't be interrupted.

"Mom. This trail is so fun. Can we splash in the creek up there when we cross it? Can I keep this pinecone?" Blaze's mouth went as fast as his legs.

"Ace, that's too big to collect," Colt warned his little brother, who was attempting to shove a shiny rock into his pocket. "Put it down and I'll find you a better one than that."

"*Awww*, Mama. Can't I keep it?" Ace bounced up to her where she was supposedly setting the hiking pace, but they were more hiking together like a squirming, breathing mass of laughter, questions, and trail snacks.

"If it fits in your pocket. If not, leave it, or the mountain will get shorter, and we'll have nothing to hike."

Ace considered this seriously, then removed a half dozen rocks from his pocket and carefully laid them on the side of the trail. He patted them before standing and catching Del's fingers in his. "There. Now the mountain will stay big and happy."

She and Del exchanged a glance. Delight shone in his eyes as he smiled approvingly at both Ace and Colt.

The tangle in her belly wasn't only physical attraction for the man. Something else was growing.

"Good job caring for the trail." Del scooped Ace up before he could stumble into the creek, then placed him on his shoulders. "Save the swimming for the pool, okay, dude?"

"Are we nearly there?" Blaze asked.

Del pointed. "Just around the corner. Come on." He checked with Stacy. "You okay if I run ahead with them and get them ready?"

"Have at it. I'll just stroll up at my leisure, then." She could already see the edge of the building, the rough rock-hewn exterior walls and green patinaed roof an eye-catching landmark.

"*Wheeeeee.*" Three boys and Del hooted as they took off and vanished up the hill.

The sun shone on her shoulders, and Stacy stopped to soak it in for a minute. This too was something she'd needed. A place far more in tune with nature. A place where stopping to take a deep inhale was encouraged.

She swung her backpack in her hand, whistling softly as she rounded the corner of the building, the one away from the parking lot and actual pool.

A young man dressed in ratty jeans and a T-shirt with a questionable graphic leaned against the nearest wall. A sneer that matched the bad attitude of his clothing marred his face.

If this had been a Toronto street-corner, Stacy would have turned around or crossed the street.

Here? He had to be a wolf. One of the Jasper pack, which meant she needed to respond accordingly.

She eyed him but kept her head high as she approached. "You plan to swim today?" she asked politely.

"'Course. All the wolves are here. Which means *you're* in the wrong place," he mumbled.

"No, I was invited."

"Maybe you're uninvited. You should leave the wolf

pack to the real wolves." Like a bad West Side Story remake, the kid peeled himself off the wall and flicked his hand downward as if opening a switchblade.

His fingers turned to claws, and his hand and arm to the elbow went furry.

What was it with these kids shifting random body parts? Seemed like a good way to cause trouble. Stacy eyed the young man, one brow raised high. "I suggest you put that away before someone gets hurt."

He grinned, and razor sharp incisors peeked out from his curled lips.

It was foolish, and foolhardy, but Stacy had reached her *enough* point, which strangely seemed to be coming sooner and sooner these days.

Then again, she'd never been one of those moms who counted to three, then four, then five, before laying down the law.

It only took one quick flash of her arm, and she'd caught hold of the brat's ear, twisting as she forced him in front of her. Yes, it was physical violence on another person's child, but the guilt factor she felt was low, considering the claw and fang issue.

Still, she kept her grip tightly controlled and focused on the claws that were way too close to her frail human body. "I don't understand why a young man like you would think this is appropriate behavior. Are you listening to me?"

"Yesh, ma'am," he lisped around his oversized fangs.

"What's your name," she demanded.

"Toby."

"Are you going to retract your claws and teeth?" She twisted his ear the slightest bit more.

"Trying. Having a hard time focuthing..." Another

lisped word, this time echoed by the embarrassment in his eyes.

"You'll be okay. Take a deep breath and hold it. That sometimes helps." She relaxed her grip. The kid wasn't really going to hurt her; he was just trying to scare her. Which was still a stupid idea, yet another example that youthful brains weren't fully formed yet, in either humans or shifters.

It took a full minute before he relaxed in her hold. "I'm sorry. I'm fully shifted now."

She turned him on the spot, still only an arm's reach away. She examined him closely, searching his face for signs that he was upset. "You okay?"

Toby's eyes widened. Then he nodded quickly and fixated on the ground. "I'm sorry," he repeated. "I had... some friends who dared me to do it."

"Don't see them around here, do you? Maybe they're not as good of friends as you thought." Stacy sniffed. "I forgive you, but don't try that again, or next time you'll be in big trouble."

He stared downward as if the ground was fascinating.

She was on a roll, so she might as well finish it. "And I'm all about personal expression and freedom of speech, but your T-shirt is obscene. It's not appropriate for young children to see, so save it to wear in places where you're around people your age or older."

"Yes, ma'am," Toby mumbled.

God, what was it with the mumbling business? "Speak up when you're spoken to. And look people in the eye."

His head snapped up. "Yes, ma'am," he said louder this time.

"Better." She patted his ear gently. "I'm sorry, too. I hope you'll forgive me for hurting you."

"It's okay. I deserved it." He looked as if he wanted to cry. "Can I... Can I have a hug?"

She hesitated, sensing the need in him, but not wanting to make a wolfish mistake. "Not sure that's a good idea. I think the scent thing might not be good if Del sniffs you on me. Right?"

The kid stepped back slightly, swallowing hard. "Oh, right. The Enforcer."

Screw it. Stacy caught Toby in a tight hug and squeezed as if he were one of her boys. "You need to chill a little. Don't hang out with kids who suggest you do things that make you uncomfortable, okay? Find some good solid wolves who are willing to stick by you even when you get in trouble. Then you'll know they're real friends."

"Okay."

She tilted her head toward the pool building. The sounds of laughter and splashing were growing louder. "I need to find my children. You going to come join us?"

His eyes lit up with eager happiness. "Sure." Toby paused. "One second." He stripped his T-shirt off over his head then put it back on inside out. "Until I'm ready to shift," he explained with a sheepish smile.

She patted him on the back then pushed him toward the pool. "That'll do. That'll do just fine."

By the time Stacy showed up, Del was waist deep in water and little boys, while wolves of all sizes excitedly leapt off the diving board and whizzed down the slide.

He waved at her as she stepped onto the deck wearing a sunshine yellow bikini top with a flared edge that covered her belly. Breasts like twin suns, lithe legs he wanted to have wrapped around him.

God, she was beautiful.

Something flew from the deck on his right and flattened Del, knocking him into the water while tangling octopus-like arms around his head. He struggled to get his feet under him, sputtering and spitting water as he stood and sucked for air.

"That was awesome," Blaze shouted, apparently the octopus. "Come on, Ace."

A second later, Del was tipping over again, conquered twice by two small boys. He was never going to live this down.

Sure enough, when he found his balance for the second time, Jace was right there, grinning at him. "I see we've found our mighty Enforcer's kryptonite."

"Small human projectile objects?" Blue suggested from his position to Jace's right.

"Minuscule amounts of yellow material." Jace danced back out of Del's reach. Ace and Blaze paddled off, eager to join Colt with the other kids and wolves setting up a game of keep away in the shallow end.

"Keep your eyes off the yellow material *and* any of her parts not covered by said fabric," Del warned.

"Oh, please. As if he's truly looking. He's got Cassidy, who would happily remove his eyeballs if he even thought about checking out another woman, especially her friend." Blue rolled his own eyes then made a considering face. "Of course, the group of single wolves over *there* are planning a mass attack on Stacy at some point. Just warning you since I set up this event as a second date for you and a certain someone—you can thank me later—and allowing anyone else to muscle in on your chance to woo said woman strikes me as silly."

Del whirled toward the corner where Blue had pointed. There was a group of twenty- and thirty-year-old guys gathered, gazes roaming the pool as they checked out the shifter women preening in sun loungers or sitting on the deck edge while doing their own not-so-discreet gazing.

Stacy settled beside Cassidy and Steph near the middle of the pool. She watched her boys with one eye and checked out the rest of the pool with the other. That her gaze drifted to Del over and over did not displease him.

The young buck slipping out of the corner did.

Del pushed past Blue and Jace. "Blue, thanks for the help. Jace, you suck. Excuse me."

"So polite," Jace snickered. "Go get her, tiger."

"That's insulting, calling him a cat," Blue complained before snickering. "Oh, I get it. Hey, Del. Go get her, meerkat."

"What the hell? A meerkat's not a *cat*," Jace drawled.

"It's not?"

The banter faded behind him as Del approached the edge of the pool in front of the ladies at the same moment the other man got there. The temptation to dunk the punk's head under the water was strong, but it wasn't the clear message Del's wolf needed to send.

And the wolf was very clearly in charge right now.

Only one thing would do. Del pushed up on the edge of the pool and rose to his feet, water streaming from his body.

Stacy's eyes widened as he walked toward her. She slammed a hand over her sister's eyes. "Del? You forgot your swimsuit."

Oh, right. He was naked. Whatever.

He didn't bother to warn off the wet-behind-the-ears

youth behind him. He just shifted between one breath and the next and continued to pace toward his future mate. One delicate jump, and he was on the end of her lounger.

He turned in a circle and settled, resting on her feet, glaring back at the young man who'd dared to approach his woman.

Sebastian held up his hands. "Okay, okay. I had no idea." He glanced at Stacy then back at Del. "I'll go over there to the corner. Far away from here. Enjoy your day, ladies. Sorry, Del. Catch you later."

"Thanks," Stephanie said, waving him off. She turned to Stacy and Cassidy, then glanced at Del. "That was cute and weird. Del, you really should warn a person before prancing around in your werewolf birthday suit. I thought Stacy was going to pass out."

"I was trying to—" Stacy sighed heavily and shook her head. "Never mind."

She dug her hands into his fur.

Del licked her nose.

Stacy laughed. "Once again, that's not a thing I'm super comfy with, wolf kissing human, which means I'm not going to analyze this moment too much."

Beside them, Cassidy smirked harder. She'd obviously figured out what was going on, the fated-mates part between Del and Stacy, whether because Cassidy was Alpha or because she and Jace had talked about it.

Still, she didn't mess things up for him. Just leaned back and looked around the pool. "Good turnout."

"It's nice to see so many of the pack in one spot." Stephanie tilted her sunglasses down and glanced over the rim. "Is it everyone?"

"No. Some will come later. Some won't come at all." Cassidy nudged Stacy and pointed to a group of ladies huddled together on the far side of the pool. "Are they the ones from the Wolf Mom Association who were giving you grief?"

Del raised his head to double-check that everyone was behaving.

Stacy scratched his ears extra hard, laughing softly as she whispered at him. "Stop growling. Everything's fine." She raised her voice. "Yes, Cass, and no. I recognize one of them, but the others are all over by the hot tub and seem to have decided to play nice. I'm not worried. The rude ones will come around eventually."

"Speaking of rude, I don't see Emma," Stephanie noted. "She's an extra special type," she warned her sister with a nod. "Blonde, used to date Jace. Thinks she's all that and a bit more, with a shitty attitude."

Stacy shrugged. "She obviously didn't get to keep Jace."

"Damn right," Cassidy muttered.

Stacy continued with a grin. "Emma's not here, having fun, soaking in the sun with her friends. I know who's smarter from that choice alone."

Stephanie chuckled. "You're right."

Conversation flowed up and down around other topics for a while as Del sat and was cuddled by Stacy in plain sight of the entire pack.

Damn, it was right to be there at her feet. To feel eyes on him and Stacy, some approving and some curious. All the pack acknowledging his claim that there was something between them.

Nothing was a done deal, but it was a very good place to start.

13

"We haven't had a girls' night out in forever." Stephanie bounced into Stacy's room, holding up two hangers with tops on them. "I know I don't need to dress up, but I want to. Which should I wear?"

With her boys happily enjoying a sleep over with Blue and Jace in Jace and Cassidy's cabin, Stacy allowed herself to wallow in the joy of a ladies-only evening.

Five days after the swimming pool date, and so far, things had been going well.

The kitchen was running smoothly with only two minor accidents. One when Jessica had tripled parts of a recipe but only doubled others, and another when Sophie had miscalculated a baking time and the three of them had to rush to fry up omelets for dinner. But Stacy was proud of her team and what they'd accomplished.

She'd had a couple more incidents in town with younger members of the wolf pack giving her attitude, but she was getting used to it. A single high dose *mom look* was usually enough to have them turning around and apologizing. Even asking for a hug.

Every night before bed, Colt excitedly shared the more advanced shifting and tracking exercises Del had begun to teach him farther away from the lodge where Stacy wasn't involved. Which meant less time seeing Del naked...

Pity, that.

Still no *talk* time with Del, either, but she'd had a couple more spectacular dreams that were tiding her over. She was more concerned about how tired he looked from dealing with the Enforcer business that had kept him away.

But tonight was not about sexual frustration but rather sisterly comradery. Not only with Steph and Cass, but a couple ladies from the pack.

"I also want to dress up because we're going to Angie's," Stephanie said. "You're going to like her. Blue took me to meet her, and she's like this kickass lawyer-helper to Del with a total take-no-shit attitude, and she dresses like a fox."

Tonight was their first time socializing, and Stacy hoped for the best, especially since she'd convinced Sophie to join them. Jessica hadn't been invited—yet. Stacy and Sophie had already become tight because of the mom angle. Jessica was...

Well, there was potential, but for now, they'd just wait and see.

"Fingers crossed it works." Stacy paused to examine her sister's choices more closely. One top was neon bright, the other pale pastels. One form fitting, one made up of flirty layers of fabric that would turn her sister into a Fae fairy. "Very different," she said. "You channeling your inner Blue?"

"What's that?" Steph flipped the tops in front of her, one then the other. "I'm not sad."

"Blue, as in your shadow. The vibrant Omega who dogs your heels if you'll excuse the pun."

"Good one, Stace. Yeah, Steph. A whole lot of neon going on there," Cassidy echoed as she marched into the room. "I like it though. You'd look good in either. Wear the bright one."

"Indecision has never been your issue," Stacy said with a smile. Cassidy wore a simple black tank top and yoga pants that showed off her toned muscles to a T. "Wow. You're looking trim these days."

"It's all the sex," Cassidy announced with zero embarrassment. "You have anything to brighten me up, without making me into a Blue clone? A scarf? A tiara?"

"I have a necklace that would go nicely with your colouring." Stacy opened the drawer of her makeup table and reached for the box where she hid the good jewelry from her boys.

A slim piece of blue paper rested on top of everything else. She pulled it out and opened it.

Careful. They're dangerous. You'll be the next one hurt.

"What's that?" Cassidy bumped her then tried to read over her shoulder. "Stace? What's going on?"

"No idea." Quickly, she folded the paper and stuck it in her pocket, glancing at her watch. "I'll ask Del to check it out later. We need to go now if we're not going to make them wait."

Cassidy gave her a look, but she didn't say anything else. Just accepted the necklace Stacy handed her then herded Steph and Stacy into the minivan the lodge had bought to replace the one that had been destroyed in the river.

They zoomed up the hill and into town, pulling to a stop outside a very nice townhouse on the end of the row, close to the edge of the woods.

Angie had a glass of wine in hand when she opened the door. "Welcome, ladies. Sophie and I are already on our second bottle. You need to catch up."

Sophie waved from her place nestled in the easy chair by the French doors to the patio. "Or not. We do have wolf metabolisms," she pointed out.

"And I have a Stephanie metabolism, which is just about as good." Steph crowded in the door and draped an arm over their shoulders from behind to do introductions. "Angie, this is my sis and my bestie. Who is also my sis's bestie, so like a second bestie. Not as in second best, but also a bestie."

"Makes sense. Maybe not after more wine, but come on in. Sisters, besties, and all. Snacks will be on the table in ten minutes. Shoes off or on, your choice. But if you take them off, let us *ooh* and *ahh* over them first."

"Deal." Cassidy twirled on the spot. "Admire me, please. Thigh high boots are not a summer fashion statement I'm trying to make trend, but damn, they're sexy. Or so Jace tells me."

"To sexy boots." Sophie raised her glass and held it there. "Hurry and start drinking. I can't toast alone."

Boots were discarded, wine was acquired.

The living room was admired. Angie's decorating style was somewhere between rustic country and copper pipe overload.

"I love the bookcase," Stacy told her as she settled on the couch next to Cassidy with her full wine glass.

"Thanks. Blue made it," Angie shared. "He's a talented man."

"Talented, and full of Omega-y goodness." Sophie wrinkled her nose and stared into her glass. "That's not right. That made him sound like a vitamin pill, and he's far too sexy to be a pill."

"To men who are talented with their hands," Angie said, lifting her glass. "And I mean that in the most platonic way possible."

"I'm sure there are a lot of the pack who meet that criteria," Stacy offered. "Not that I'm looking," she hurried to add.

Angie outright grinned. "Because you're not interested or because you've already picked your mark?"

The best way to answer that was to ignore it, Stacy decided.

Wine flowed. Food came out. A cheesy dip and crispy salty chips. Small meatballs in a savoury barbeque sauce. Angie explained a little more about what she did for Delaney's business (basically everything, including forging his name when necessary), and Sophie told more stories about pack shenanigans. Cassidy had them all in stitches doing a re-enactment of her former boss getting caught peeping into a suite by a very influential politician in said room with someone who was *not* his official partner.

Stacy was nice and relaxed, and when it was her turn to have the floor, she had a question in mind. "Do I have some kind of *time to challenge the new human in town* sticker on my back? Or am I being hazed? I've had a half dozen teens, maybe a little older, partially shift in front of me. They all have bad attitudes or tons of sass, that sort of thing."

"They're pulling power moves on you," Angie explained with a wise nod. "Hope you've had fun putting them in their place."

Serious thoughts flew. Far too serious considering the amount of alcohol in her system.

"Power moves. Like testing to see what they can get

away with?" Cassidy demanded, incensed on Stacy's behalf.

"Some. Maybe testing to see what she *won't* let them get away with." Angie eyed Stacy. "Gut response, take it or leave it, they see Del's interest in you, and they wonder if you're the other half."

Staring at the woman wasn't the right response, but Stacy's jaw was on the floor and there wasn't anything she could do other than gasp. "What other half?"

"Leadership team. Like Jace and Cassidy." Angie faced her straight on. "Wolves like to know where they sit in the hierarchy. They also like to know they have a solid place to stand. People to guard them, people to care for them."

Oh boy. So much became clear in a rush. People saw her and Del as a pair already? Which...the tangled feelings sweeping through her needed to be poked and considered privately.

So she used her prize-winning topic-segueing skills once again. "Thanks for the reminder. That hierarchy nonsense." Stacy faced Sophie. "You make me crazy. You're so much better in the kitchen now, and here—I know Angie is a strong wolf, yet you tease her. Why do you let the other pack ladies run you down so often?"

"Agreed. I don't get it either. I suppose I get the power part, but they're *mean* to you. Why do you put up with that?" Cassidy asked Sophie.

The young woman shrugged. "I'm near the bottom of the totem pole, but I also think the mean girls are jealous. I've got a beautiful little girl, I have good friends, so I feel sorry for them. Plus, my wolf doesn't like conflict, so it's easier to grovel the few times when the mean girls and I interact."

"Where's Dixie on the dominance scale? Doesn't it

make it harder for her when her mama doesn't stand up for herself?"

Angie grinned. "That's part of the problem. Dixie is a little powerhouse, so Sophie isn't worried about her, are you darling?"

Sophie smiled. "My baby can take care of herself."

So very confusing. "I really wish you'd also take care of yourself." Stacy told her gently.

"I'm trying." Sophie stared into her wine before looking up and offering a brilliant smile. "It's been nice to work with you. You make it easier to do my job *and* work on being strong."

"Lots of things are about power when it comes down to it." Angie shrugged. "You need to figure out how you want to deal with it, and then the rest gets easier."

"People need to do their jobs. That makes life easier too."

"Speaking of doing our jobs." Cassidy held out her hand. "Give me that note you found."

Stacy passed it over without thinking. "Why?"

"Because I'm your Alpha, that's why."

Stacy rolled her eyes the way her boys would have. "Geez, that's annoying. As bad as *because I'm the mom.*"

"Exactly." Cassidy eyed the words again, then folded it up and held it toward Angie. "Don't read it. Do you have any idea who touched this other than Stacy and me?"

Angie's brow rose. "You want me to sniff it?"

"Yeah, but I still think that sounds rude to ask." Cassidy grinned. "I'll get over it eventually."

With a laugh, Angie lifted the note to her nose. One slow inhale later, she smiled. "Hints of cinnamon, chocolate, and raspberries."

Stephanie snickered into her wine glass. "A very fine year?"

The older woman shrugged and handed the note back to Cassidy. "A very fine cook. This smells like both Sophie and Stacy. What was for dessert at the Lodge tonight?"

Drat. "Raspberry torte. All you smell is me." Which meant Stacy would give the message to Del as she'd planned and let him deal with it. "Speaking of dessert, I brought the leftovers. Anybody want some?"

A chorus of cheers rang out, and mysterious messages and power lessons were forgotten as sugar flowed as freely as the wine.

Only Stacy had a lot to think about, and a lot to ask Del...very soon.

ONE DEAD END AFTER ANOTHER. That was all Del had found after following every lead he had related to the discovery in the bowling alley.

He waved goodbye to the family he'd been visiting, ignored the straight route to his house in town, and headed on foot back to Timberwolf Lodge.

The sweet adventure with Stacy and her boys a few days earlier had faded to memory, and he craved more time with them.

No matter what, he'd made sure to be there for Colt's daily lessons. The kid was amazing and an eager learner, and Del enjoyed the time with him immensely. The glimpses Del saw of Stacy were tantalizing, and he stole them because not getting to see her made his wolf itch. But the time with Colt was a reward in itself.

He missed Ace and Blaze though, which also told him a

ton about what was going on with his wolf and how much his plans needed to be accelerated.

The upside was he'd been able to deal with one dangerous issue in a timely manner. The kid from the bowling alley who had been working the day they'd gone, Carter Simmons, had come to Del a few days later, looking for help.

"I don't feel right," Carter admitted. "I'm...picking fights. And not just with my brothers, which would make sense because they're family and we're supposed to mess around, but with adults and wolves I know better than to poke." He lifted his gaze quickly then dropped it. "I was rude to Stacy and her boys when they were at the alley. I didn't mean to be, it just blurted out, as if someone else was talking for me."

The drugs, Del realized. "You might have gotten a bit of something that's messing with your shifter system, completely by accident," he assured the kid. "Let me call Blue, and we'll help you."

Help which consisted mostly of him and Blue spending time with Carter, letting his wolf know he had a solid place in the pack and didn't need to fight to move up the hierarchy. Blue might have done something else more magical, but for Del, the job mostly consisted of taking Carter for a couple of long runs as wolves and then playing a whole bunch of wild and exuberant board games with the whole set of Simmons boys.

Spending time enjoying the family bonds that were clearly there between the young men only made the urge to be with Stacy and her boys more intense.

Del jogged a little faster, the need to be near them strengthening until it was a pounding ache inside. He was still waiting for information from Toronto regarding

Dwight, and he'd put out a request for as much information as possible regarding James. All the people from Stacy's past who might be able to offer information to make her future safer.

But now it was time to settle himself down enough to rest so he could start all over the next day. He paused at the edge of the cleared lawn that surrounded Timberwolf lake. Stripping off his clothes, he stashed them in one of the camouflaged shelving units they'd built for that purpose.

He shifted, then ran.

Some nights when he did a perimeter sweep, Jace or Blue joined him. Or both, the three of them building their team in ways instinctive to all wolves. Dashing around trees, scrambling up rock faces. Occasionally pushing each other into rose bushes—

They were as bad as Carter and his brothers in some ways.

Which meant they were also *good* in the same way as brothers. Their connection was one of choice, not blood. The binding together of powerful men to make the pack better for the many under them. A responsibility that Del had taken seriously as Alpha. A responsibility he took seriously now.

But Blue and Jace made it more than it had been before. It was still a huge task, but now laughter and games and heart and hope were tangled up in being leaders.

Part of that was Cassidy, Del knew. Her touch had strengthened Jace, and so strengthened the pack. Stacy was already building ties to the pack...

Even unknowingly, which only made her more amazing in his books.

Nothing was a given yet, but he wanted her so badly he couldn't imagine a future without her and the boys.

He'd run for long enough that night had truly fallen. She'd be home from her night with Angie and her girls, and hopefully asleep. The lodge would be quiet and still, and no one would notice his arrival.

Del sprinted the final way to the lodge then shifted, chest still heaving as he eyed the building and considered where he should crash for the night. One of the empty cabins was the most logical choice.

Don't want logic. Want to be with Stacy, his wolf informed him firmly.

So be it.

A little manoeuvering was necessary, and the use of his claws, but he clambered up the side of the house and made it to the balcony outside Stacy's second story suite without breaking a sweat. The fact he'd done it so easily added another item to his *upgrades to security* to-do list.

The window was open, and her scent drifted out to him. The fainter aroma of the boys in the background meshed with hers perfectly, so clearly a family, that he found himself smiling.

All of them are mine.

Not yet, he warned his wolf, *but soon.*

The curtains waved in the breeze, the faintest moonlight overhead shining in to land on her sleeping form. Curled up on her side, her face caressed with silver light, she was a goddess and a Madonna all in one.

Satisfied that they were all where they were supposed to be, Del shifted. He curled up on the patio and closed his eyes, the small sounds of the forest at night washing over him. His muzzle rested on his paws, the wooden deck boards under his belly still warm from the summer sunshine.

Moments later? Hours? He dreamed he was walking as

a human, hand in hand with Stacy beside the lake in the fading light of evening.

She tucked her hair behind her ear and smiled at him. "You're a hard man to track down these days."

"You should ask Colt to help. He's got an excellent sixth sense at figuring out when I'm pulling a fast one and doubling back on the trail."

"He's so excited by all the things you're teaching him." She squeezed his fingers. "Blaze and Ace want to know when they get to have wolf lessons with you. Which—don't worry, they know that they can't actually shift. They just want to spend time with you."

"They're great kids." He pulled her to a stop beside the rustic log bench Blue had positioned overlooking the lake and the sunset. "They've got a great mom."

"Why, thank you, sir. Are you sweet-talking me?" She batted her lashes at him. "I hope so."

"I was hoping for talking, and some *talking*," he admitted, sitting then pulling her between his legs. She stood with her back to the lake, the bright colours of sunset glowing around her head like a halo.

Vibrant, yet steely strong. She examined him carefully. One hand touched his forehead, tracing it smooth before she stroked the back of her knuckles down his cheek. "I want to *talk* so much," she agreed.

A second later, she'd straddled his thigh, her legs wide over his. Her hands drifted down his chest, lower, lower...

Eyes still in direct contact with his, she undid the button on his slacks and lowered the zipper.

"Stace," he whispered. Was it a protest or a request that she absolutely continue her trek?

She raised a brow. "The last time we *talked*, which I will now call fooling around for a reason I'll share later, I remember doing a lot of begging for you to stop teasing. My turn."

"I've created a monster," Del said before she stole the power of speech from him along with the rest of the blood in his brain.

Her hand around his cock, cool and smooth, was utter perfection.

No, wait. Her hand around his cock, *stroking* him, was perfection.

She pressed upward on her knees far enough to nuzzle her lips against his neck, nibbling and kissing and sucking lightly. The entire time, that hand of hers drove him wild. He closed his eyes and let pleasure wash over him, anticipation swelling. The tingles in his balls and lower spine danced small electrical volts of extra-charged debauchery.

He wanted this. Wanted her.

She sat back, pausing her motion, stealing a groan from him as he bit his lip to keep from demanding she continue.

Her eyes were bright and focused. "Del?"

"Stace?"

"Del." Firmer now, a frown on her face instead of pleasure. "Wake up."

14

Feeling this much was dangerous, Stacy decided.

It couldn't be healthy for her heart to race this hard, or her body to ache so much, or every one of her nerve endings to be sensitized to the breaking point.

She'd walked with Del under the sunlit sky and flirted. Then she'd taken the bull by the horns, so to speak, *cough, cough,* and crawled into his lap.

Giving Del pleasure was indescribable. Starting at a personal orgasm level then shooting beyond, connecting physically, and seeing how much he wanted her, wanted her touch—

Incredible.

Until...

Something clicked. *Blurred.*

He was still there, under her hands, her lips on his body, but it wasn't *true.*

It's a dream.

The voice inside her head was enough to spin her into sitting upright in her bed. Eyes open, taking in the curtains wavering in the breeze, the firm mattress under her hips and hand.

A dream?

Yes, another dream, but so real and intense, and still lingering on the edges of her vision. As if she had a channel in her mind she could tune in a little sharper if she wanted to and refocus. Be right back there with Del.

Or I could stay awake and grab the living, breathing man.

Stacy threw back the quilt and paced instinctively across the floor to the French doors. She pulled the right one open and found Del in his wolf form, partially curled up on the soft blanket that had fallen off the lounger.

"Del?"

"Stace?"

She gasped in a breath. That was *Del's* voice inside her head. Things were officially beyond incredible and veering into outright miraculous.

"Del." How on earth was she supposed to deal with him as a wolf? "Wake up," she said sharply.

He wiggled slightly, then sighed and seemed to go back to sleep.

Frustrated now, she poked him with her toes.

Instant reaction. The wolf jerked upright to all four paws, fully alert and staring at her.

"Come inside," she ordered.

Del paced in, pausing until she closed the door. He stared, and she swore he was thinking hard enough for her to hear it.

"Fine." She locked the deadbolt.

He turned, jumped up on her bed, and settled to his belly. His intense stare seemed both possessive and worried.

"I don't mind, but if I'm going to be honest, as much as I like your wolf, I'd prefer the human Del in my bed."

Between one breath and the next, he shifted. Stretched out, one knee bent up, reclined on his side like a model. "Better?"

"Much." She fanned her face, refusing to look away. In fact, she looked her fill. "Holy moly, Del. You make it tough to concentrate on the important questions. Like, what on earth is going on?"

"Were you having another very, very good dream?" Del asked.

"I was, and I think you were having one, too."

"It did not suck," he agreed. "Waking up? That's a toss-up right now. I hated it for a while, but there's the potential for me to really like where this is going."

Heat washed over her. Not embarrassment, but aching need. Still, Stacy paused and thought back to everything that she'd learned since arriving in Jasper.

Her friend Cassidy now had a wolf shifter for a partner. Fated mates she'd called it. As if they belonged together and had always meant to be. But Cassidy had also fully chosen it.

Del had done nothing but stick to Stacy's side since the moment they'd met and done everything to be there for her and the boys. He'd said...

She struggled to recall his exact words, but mostly remembered the part about finding a way to date her while staying on the non-creepy stalker side.

Angie said the pack thought they were a part of the leadership team. Not just Del, but Del *and* Stacy.

As much as she wanted to simply pick up where the dream had left off, she wanted this more. She wanted to know. To understand.

To be able to choose, like Cassidy had, her own future.

"I need to ask you three things," Stacy blurted out.

His lips twisted into a smile as he teased. "Disappointing. Here I thought we'd established that our version of *talking* was a tactile endeavor. Still, I'm game." Del curled upright on the mattress and sat cross-legged.

Stacy stared at the ceiling for moment while willing her blood pressure back to normal. She snatched up her pillow and tossed it in his lap.

He smirked.

"Humour the human," she said dryly.

Curiosity grew in his expression. "We've had a three-part conversation before."

"I know. I like traditions." Only where to start? The reminder of the first discussion was the answer. "When we started, when we actually had a good long talk that involved words, you said you wouldn't drop everything on me at one time. The wolf stuff."

"Is that a question?"

"No, this is. You and I, dating. Being together. We're not just an interlude, are we?"

"No, we're not an interlude. Not for me." The sheer relief in saying the words was so immense Del could have collapsed to the mattress like a puddle of wolf pudding. But he had to tell it all. "You haven't truly decided to be with me, though. And until you do, nothing is set in stone."

She lifted her hand and a second finger. "Am I supposed to be part of the leadership team of the Jasper pack?"

"Yes." He said it instantly, no holding back. "Everything

about you and how the pack reacts to you makes that crystal clear. The things they tell you, the smartass tests they pull, all big signs that they're trying to figure out how much you'll put up with, even while hoping the answer is *not much.*"

Stacy frowned. "Really?"

"Really." He lifted his hands in the air. "Think of your boys. Would they really be happy if you let them stay up late every night, eat crap, and never brush their teeth? Or do they not so secretly adore that you instinctively know when they simply stuck their toothbrush under the water and then put it back in the holder without using it."

She snorted. "Blaze tried that three days in a row with escalating levels of pseudo-brushing. When Colt teased him because Blaze was taking longer to pretend to brush his teeth than to simply brush them, things got sorted out."

"And that's part of why they love you so much. You know what they're up to. Sometimes you lay down the law, and sometimes you let someone near and dear to them be the hammer." Del caught her fingers in his. "Jasper pack needs different people to be different things to run as a cohesive unit. Jace and Cassidy are Alphas now. They're the solid base for the rest to stand on. The strength and the power to do what needs to be done."

"But you're the Enforcer. Doesn't that mean your job is also about power?"

"Yes, but a different kind. Think less like a warrior and more like a peacekeeper. *Enforcing* the rules in the best way possible."

Her mouth hung open. "I'd thought of it all wrong. I'd assumed your job was to be the muscle."

He shrugged. "I can be when I need to be." Del smiled. "Very much like you. You're no pushover when you're in Mama bear mode, are you?"

She shook her head in disbelief. "No. But you do realize this means that you're a Mama bear too. You're so good with the boys and with the other pack members I've seen you with. They look up to you and want to please you. You encourage them to be better by letting them be their best selves."

"I hope that's the case. But let's not use that phrase *mama bear* anywhere Blue can hear, okay? I don't need to be asked from now to eternity if my porridge is too hot or too cold."

Stacy pressed a hand to her chest. "This is making a lot more sense now. As much as the talking has been down a different path than our dreams led us."

Del didn't want to push too hard. "I'm still here, and the night isn't over."

"No, it's not." Her expression was still too thoughtful to be the *please ravish me now* he was hoping for. "Ready for my final question?"

"Maybe."

She patted his knee. "Don't worry. Too much."

He snorted.

Stacy lifted her hand again and revealed three fingers. "If we're fated mates, and if I'm already a part of the pack leadership, I'm going to consider it really hard, but I need more time."

"That wasn't really a question," he pointed out, amusement waging a war with disappointment. "I mean, grammatically you did use the word *if* a couple of times, but you mostly made a statement."

"Wow, an active member of the grammar police. Now I know another task on your Enforcer job list," she teased before offering a sad smile. "And you're right. I made a statement—I need more time. It's been less than two weeks since I arrived in Jasper. So my question is, can you forgive me for needing to be sure?"

Oh God. "*Stace.* There's nothing to forgive."

Del had reached his limit, unable to remain beside her and not touch. He needed to reassure her that anything she needed was important to him. Any worry or sadness, he would go to war to change.

He scooped her into his lap and cradled her close. "I want you. That is the truth and will not change. But I want you, *all* of you, willing and open and completely choosing to be by my side for the rest of our lives. That's more important to me than you can know."

"Thank you," she whispered, true relief evident. She cupped his cheek, tilting his face toward her. She stared at him as if she could read his soul, and a hint of worry returned. "What happened? What did you have to do that you wouldn't have chosen to do?"

It *had* only been two weeks, Del realized. He'd been so caught up in knowing his mate was here in Jasper that he'd ignored all the other important parts, like sharing who he was and what had come before to make him this way.

"I didn't want to be Alpha," he admitted. "Before Jace took over, the night you arrived, I was Alpha for the pack. You knew that, right?"

She nodded. "Cassidy said you took over for your Dad."

Del cringed involuntarily. "Took over is a...mild word for it." He met her gaze, hoping against hope to not lose her forever with his confession. "My dad got hooked on a drug that messes with shifter hormones. He was already Alpha for the pack, but it made him want to be *more*. More powerful, more in charge, more instantly obeyed."

"A dictator instead of a leader like Jace and Cassidy?"

"Yes, and dangerous. He hurt one of the teenagers of the pack who he said was being disrespectful. The kid hadn't seen him, was just hanging out and fooling around, and my Dad beat him so badly that Joey ended up in the hospital."

Stacy pressed a hand to her mouth. "Oh my God."

"Joey's okay," Del assured her. "But he no longer lives here. I found him a new home in an Edmonton pack, and he's doing well."

She vibrated in his arms. "Tell me the rest."

Straightforward was the only way. "Dad had become dangerous to the pack. The kids, the babies— We couldn't let it continue. And the strongest wolf in the pack, the one to confront him, was..."

He couldn't say it.

Stacy stroked his cheek. "You?"

"Jace."

Her eyes widened with shock.

Del pressed on. "But Jace had spent years of education and every penny he'd saved to get Carter Wells up and running. It's a system that creates affordable, safe water for remote communities, and he was on the verge of making it a reality when Dad went off the rails."

"Oh, Del."

Her expression made it clear she'd made the leap and already connected the dots, but he finished it anyway. "If Jace had become Alpha, he'd have been stuck here, and he needed to leave to complete his project. It makes a big difference to a lot of people, and it wouldn't have happened without him at the helm at least until it got off the ground. I'd already gotten my legal training and was back in Jasper to stay. So while I wasn't the strongest, I was strong enough.

I removed the threat and became Alpha in my father's place. Then because he was still stronger, I had to go all asshole on Jace. I told him to leave town or else. Thank God, he took the out, but it meant suddenly I was alone with a job I didn't want, but one the pack desperately needed me to do."

"So you became Alpha instead of Enforcer as you should have." She nodded slowly. "I see why you understand the importance of being allowed to make a choice."

He had to know. "Stacy. You still want to be with me? After hearing what I did?"

She blinked, confused for a moment before understanding dawned. "The part where you took out a dangerous man to protect the innocent? Del." She laid her head on his chest. "You just explained how we're the mama bears of the pack. You think I wouldn't kill to protect my boys? Even if it was someone who had once been close to me?"

"I hope you never have to, but...you're right. You're fierce, and gentle, and strong, and sweet, and everything I want." Relief hit so strong and hard that he swayed on the spot. "Thank you."

"What a pair we are," she whispered. "Kind of perfect for each other."

They stayed like that for a while longer, clinging to each other. Then Del pushed her gently toward her pillow. "Let's get under the covers," he suggested. "I need to stay and hold you. Nothing more right now. Just let me hold you."

She nodded, exhaustion on her face. But her eyes were clear and bright, and she seemed content to curl up in his arms, face-to-face. Limbs tangled, hands linked.

It wasn't sex, but it was still very intimate.

His wolf settled, peaceful for the first time in months. Del fell asleep with his mate in his arms and the promise of a forever somewhere ahead of them.

15

———

*L*ight was stealing between the curtain, and a warm, lush woman was curled up against him. Del's body was fully awake even if his brain wasn't. Or at least his cock was awake, firm and firmly tucked against Stacy's sweet backside.

He hummed happily when he realized that sometime during the night she'd rolled and tucked into him like the little spoon, and how not only was he pressed to her ass, but his left hand cupped her breast. "Please tell me you're awake."

"Awake, but about to warn you that even though my thoughts are going the same direction as yours—"

The foot of the mattress bounced. Once, twice, three times.

"*Maaaaaaama.*" Ace scrambled over their legs. Del instinctively rolled tighter to Stacy to keep the delicate portions of his anatomy from being stepped on. Another wiggle, and the kid was straddling Del and Stacy's ribs, looking down with delight in his eyes. "You had a sleepover!"

Oh shit.

Thank goodness, Stacy laughed.

She twisted, wiggled back to a sitting position and scooped Ace up in her arms. "We did. How are you guys this morning? Did you catch any invading aliens in your sleep?"

"I dreamed about hamburgers," Blaze announced, forcefully pushing his way into Del's lap. "I'm hungry."

"Makes sense," Del said before pulling on a horrified expression. "Your pillow isn't missing, is it? You didn't eat it in the middle of the night?"

Blaze snickered. "I dreamed about hamburgers, not marshmallows. Everyone knows you only eat your pillow after dreaming about marshmallows."

"Oh. I stand corrected." Del met the eyes of the wolf still perched at the foot of the bed. "Morning, Colt."

Colt dipped his head, his gaze darting between Del and his mom. Yeah, he was old enough to know this wasn't an innocent sleepover situation.

Stacy was aware as well, in the *eyes in the back of her head* way all moms had. Even as she cuddled Ace and listened to his list of everything he was going to do that day, she motioned Colt forward.

He stepped delicately to the space right between the two of them.

"I'd like Del to give you your lesson this morning," she told Colt. "Tonight, Del and I are going on a date, so he won't be able to work with you then. Okay?"

Colt shifted, a small pale human with wide eyes. "You're going on a date?"

"Can we come?" Ace asked. "Are you going bowling again?"

"You're going to have to stay at Timberwolf Lodge," Stacy informed him. "This date is for grown-ups only."

"That's dumb," Blaze announced before frowning at Del. "Why do you want to have a date with just Mom? She can't do cannonballs nearly as good as we can."

Talk about out of the frying pan and into the fire. Del glanced at Stacy, hoping for a clue of what direction she wanted this to go.

No help there. She looked hugely amused as if interested to see what he'd say.

Del focused on the three sets of questioning eyes on him now. He test-drove sentences in his brain, rejecting them one after another. *Your mom and I want to see if we like each other* was too mild and too wrong to say out loud. *We're mates* was too far the other way.

Fine. Stick with one truth. "I plan to kiss your Mom, a lot, and that would probably be boring for you guys."

Ace shrugged. "I kiss mama a lot. See?" He lifted and planted one on her. A wet, little-boy smack that rang loud and clear. Then he turned to Del and kissed him as well before dropping off the bed and racing back toward the room he shared with Blaze. "I need to find my cars."

"Hey, Del, do you know how a wolf eats breakfast?" Blaze had already ignored the date issue and was backing toward the door. "He wolves it down." With a hyena laugh, he twisted and chased after Ace. "Don't touch my trucks."

And then there was one. Colt had wrapped his arms around his skinny little legs and was staring intently at his mom.

She lifted a brow. "Yes?"

He glanced at Del then back at Stacy. "Mom, you're not a wolf."

"Nope, I'm not." She waited patiently as Colt struggled to find the right words.

Join the club, Del thought. Talking about shit was tough.

Colt nodded quickly, glanced at Del, then took a deep breath. "Del's been teaching me about trusting my wolf. How I need to say stuff when my wolf pokes me to. You don't have a wolf, so sometimes I need to say things for you, too, I think."

"Oh, sweetie. You're my little boy. I'm responsible for you, not the other way around."

He shook his head, hard. "It's not that. Just...with *him*. Blaze's daddy. He wasn't right."

Del stilled. "What do you mean?"

Colt lifted his chin. "He didn't hurt me, or Blaze. But he wasn't *right*. Like he was pretending to be someone he wasn't. So my wolf helped me, and we never let him see that I could shift. I know I was littler then, but I remember. My wolf told me we had to keep it a secret, so we did."

The three of them sat on the bed with the sun pouring in the curtains and an icy chill in the air.

Beside him, Stacy reached for Colt's hands. "You're right. Porter wasn't who he said he was, so I'm very glad your wolf helped you stay secret. But that man is no longer anyone we need to worry about. The part he *was* right for was giving me your brothers. They are exactly who I'd always wanted to have join you and me."

"They're *mine*," Colt declared firmly. "They're not wolves, but they're my pack. And so are you." He crawled into her lap a little more awkwardly than Ace had. All long limbs and coltish like his namesake.

Del felt a fierce shot of pride. "Good job, buddy."

Colt met his gaze, more wolf in his eyes than human. "*You're* right. I mean, my wolf says you're *right*. For mom, for me and Blaze and Ace." Colt tipped his head back and focused on Stacy. "He says you needed to know that."

Sweet, unexpected backup from the most unexpected of sources.

Stacy kissed Colt's nose. "Thank you for sharing. Your wolf is very smart."

"He wants us all to be together. Can we be? For real?"

A small laugh escaped her. "Nothing like a little extra pressure. Well, Colt, Del told me this morning that he and I are mates. But since, as you pointed out, I'm human, I need a little longer to wrap my head around it. So Del and I are going to date."

Colt frowned. "But you're mates. Like Cassidy and Jace?"

"Yes, but first, we date. Got it?" Stacy said firmly. "Now you need to go brush your teeth and get ready for breakfast."

"Don't bother with breakfast," Del added. "We're going hunting."

"Okey dokey. Still, brush your teeth, and then you can enjoy your...bunnies or whatever." Stacy wrinkled her nose.

A snicker escaped Colt as he wiggled off the bed. "You're funny. You cook meat all the time."

"Key word there, kiddo. *Cook.* Now go. Del will be out in a minute."

"Don't bother dressing, either. Meet me on the front porch," Del told him.

Colt scrambled to the door, paused, then whirled to face them. "It's not just my wolf," he said seriously. "*I* want us to be together."

Stacy blew him a kiss. He vanished.

Well, that had been a thing.

Del scooped Stacy up and kissed her thoroughly,

nipping at her lower lip until she opened with a gasp. Teasing his tongue over hers. By the time he pulled back, they were both breathless and Stacy's cheeks were glowing pink.

"Nice icing on the cake," she told him.

"Kids add an element to life, don't they?"

She eyed him closely. "You're getting not just a mate, but a family."

"I wouldn't want it any other way," he told her with full honesty. "But first, we date. Remember?"

Her smile lit up the room and suddenly the cold was gone, and all Del could see was a clear path ahead to happiness.

STACY STOOD on the porch and watched as her son and her... Boyfriend? Future mate?...took off into the trees. Colt's nose was down and his tail up, and he was just about the most adorable thing she'd ever seen.

Smart kid. Amazing kid. *My wolf has things to tell you.* God, her heart nearly exploded at what he'd shared.

Which meant it was time to get this show on the road, but no more traveling without a map.

She raced upstairs, positioned herself outside her sister's room, and banged loudly as she shouted at the top of her lungs. "Stephanie. Get your butt downstairs, stat." Stacy pulled out her phone and messaged Cassidy even as she shouted a second and final warning. "I mean it, Steph. I'm coming in there with a bucket of cold water in two minutes if you're not at the kitchen table by then."

Stacy slipped over to her suite and peeked in on Ace and Blaze, but they were happily engaged in building an epic racetrack for their Hot Wheels. She closed the door silently, went downstairs and put on coffee, because she wasn't some kind of heathen who demanded important wake-up conversations with her girls without providing java.

Three minutes later a bright-eyed Cassidy strolled in the kitchen door while Stephanie, with uncombed hair and crumpled pink baby doll pyjamas, stumbled her way to the table.

Stacy placed a large mug of coffee in front of each of them, and a plate of cookies in front of herself.

Her sister lifted the mug to her lips and groaned at the scent of it. "You suck, but I already forgive you because...caffeine."

Cassidy smiled at Steph then lifted her mug in a salute to Stacy. "Our early-morning emergency meeting is now in session." She eyed the cookies. "You plan to hand those over as rewards for good behavior?"

"Yup."

Cassidy blinked. "Oh. I was kidding."

"I'm not," Stacy informed them. "We are having an emergency meeting, and the sooner you both confess all, the better."

Steph looked confused, but Cassidy's expression leaned toward guilt, which was pretty much what Stacy had expected. She faced her friend. "Did you know that Del and I are mates?"

Cassidy swung a triumphant fist in the air. "*Yes*. I am so happy—"

"Potential mates," Stacy clarified. "It's not a done deal."

Her friend froze in mid-swing and made a face. "Well, shit." She sat back in her chair. "No cookies for me, right?"

"No cookies for you." Stacy turned to her sister, who

was trying hard to figure out what had just happened. "Here's the situation, Steph. We are surrounded by a pack of wolf shifters. Cassidy, it turns out, has a magical connection to Jace that now means she is co-ruler of the whole ungainly mess."

"Hey, they're not that messy," Cassidy complained.

"Stow it, Alpha." Stacy winked, though, and passed over a cookie. Cassidy lifted it in the air in a salute as Stacy continued. "Del is also a wolf shifter, and wolves have fated mates, and I am the lucky lady Del's wolf has fallen for."

Stephanie frowned. "You and Del just started dating."

"And we're going to continue to date for a while, but it appears the magical, mystical *woo-woo* stuff has struck again, and this time, I'm it."

"It's not so terrible," Cassidy assured her. "The fated mate part. Jace and I might have been meant to be, but it's also the rightest thing I've ever felt. Kind of like when lightning strikes and—"

Stephanie laughed. "Cass, your analogies suck." She looked Stacy in the face, examining her carefully. "Are you okay with this? Having a guy back in your world? Because I know you've been hurt in the past..."

"Oh, sweetie." Stacy took her sister's hand. "I was sad and upset when James died. And I was hurt by Porter's betrayal. But I'm smart enough to know that it's not wrong to want to move ahead. It's not wrong to want a man to love. I've got you two, and I'm so grateful for all you've done over the years. But Del feels right. Like Cassidy said."

"Okay, then." Steph dipped her chin. "So let me get this straight. You woke us up to say that you are not yet, but potentially will be mates with Del, but you're still going to date. Which is mostly where you were at when we went to sleep."

"Yes."

Her sister glared at her. She snatched the plate of cookies out from under Stacy's fingers and picked the biggest one from the pile. "Meany. Don't wake us up just to tell us what we already know."

Stacy laughed. "That wasn't the emergency. This is— I'm taking Del out tonight. Where are we going, and will you two take care of the boys? Also, next week the kitchen is attempting a trial run for our first Timberwolf Lodge tasting menu, and I need you both there, plus a list of guests. Who do we ask? And I need your help to narrow down the menu because Sophie, Jessica, and I can't decide."

"Well, that's easy. Of course, we'll help." Cookie crumbs scattered as Steph snapped her teeth into one of the sweet treats.

Cassidy nodded, but she also lowered her voice and apologized. "I'm sorry I didn't say anything specific about you and Del being mates sooner. I only sort of knew that *maybe* it was a possibility. That's why Del was acting weird around you, Steph. You know, the sniffing thing."

What? Stacy eyed her sister. "Del was sniffing around *you?*"

"Don't get your panties in a twist. He wasn't *sniffing around*, just...literally sniffing. Around." She did an imitation of a blood hound, rounding the corner of the table as she did so. She stuck her nose into Stacy's hair and sniffed extra hard a couple more times.

Stacy laughed and pushed her away. "Stop it. That's rude."

"That's what I said." Steph held up a fist. "Time to get to work. Power triplets, activate."

"Zippy." From Cassidy.

"Zapp-i-roni." Stephanie with a grin.

"Zoom." Fist bumps, ready for action. Stacy eyed her friends, and contentment stole in for the first time in a long time. She had a place where she was needed. Her children were happy and safe and growing up surrounded by love. She had a man who knew to hold her when she was needy.

It was time to rock his wolfish socks off.

$\mathcal{D}$el stood in Jace's cabin and adjusted his collar. He usually loved his fancy suits. Loved how he felt in them, and he knew he looked good, but as much as he wanted to be sharp for his date with Stacy, something seemed off.

"Is this what I should be doing when we're still not sure it's completely safe?" Del demanded. "What about the stranger asking about Stacy? What about the note she found in her drawer? What about the drugs?"

Jace sighed. "I've been all over Jasper with a fine-tooth comb. Plus my sniffer, and *your* sniffer, and *Blue's* sniffer. There hasn't been a single trace of the drug anywhere."

"But we smelled it."

"We did, but whoever bought it made that one slip, and now they're either far from town or they're being uber-careful. We have to assume that they'll mess up again sometime, and probably soon." Jace let an evil grin take over his expression. "No one can touch that stuff without delusions of grandeur going to their heads. At some point, they'll push the wrong person around, and we'll know who's getting too big for their britches."

"Plus, you said the Toronto pack tracked Dwight down and they're keeping an eye on him. He's still at home, not going anywhere. So ignore him for the moment." Blue flipped through the ties he'd dumped on the bed and made a face. "You have terrible taste in clothing, dude. They're all blue. Or black. Or blue with black."

"I know," Del said with mock sadness, reaching past his cousin for the tie he wanted. "We can't all shine like neon stars."

Blue twisted to face him, eyeing him closely. "You're taunting me." He glanced at Jace. "Is he taunting me?"

"No, he's absolutely serious." Jace and Del exchanged eye rolls. "Why are you so worried, Del? You know Stacy is mostly in love with you already."

"Not so much nervous as I want to get this right. She deserves to feel like she's precious, and I want to make up for all the sad moments she's faced in the past." Del patted his tie smooth then glanced to the side where Jace and Blue had both gone silent. "What? Too emo for you guys?"

Blue crossed the cabin floor, and all traces of his casual *whatever* attitude vanished. He stood there for a moment then nodded. "Okay. I like you again."

Jace snorted. "Because it's all about whether or not Blue likes you."

"It is," Blue insisted, hand pressed to his chest. He leaned toward Jace and spoke in an eerie tone. "Have you not heard of the curse of the Omega wolf? Not a thing you'd want to mess with, my dear cousin."

"You're so much bullshit and beans," Jace muttered, but he also eyed Del. "And you, take a deep breath and enjoy yourself. We've got things covered."

"Oh, wait. I have a present for you two. Because magical Omega, yada, yada." Blue pulled a small Bluetooth speaker from his pocket and placed it in Del's palm. "You can thank me later. Oh, and I emailed you a playlist. Make sure you upload it right away and have it handy."

"Thanks." Del nodded at them, the small bud of happiness inside finally tilting toward maybe, *maybe* being a sure thing. Ready to grow into full flower.

He poked at his phone as he crossed the lawn to the lodge, pausing to let technology do its thing. As he stood there, he admired all the improvements that had been made over the past weeks. The dozen cabins were all scrubbed and tidy, with solid new roofs and eavestroughs. The lodge itself had been power washed, and the old log beams shone with honey-gold tones that reflected the sunlight.

The lawn was mowed perfection, with a firepit area *here* and a row of sun loungers *there*. The dock out over the water held a small table and umbrella, which seemed a strange place for it. Pretty, but odd.

"Hello, stranger." Stacy stood on the back porch, happiness shining in her eyes. She wore a green sundress with happy yellow polka dots. Bright, but not blinding like Blue's usual outfits. Just...pretty.

Del held out the flowers he'd picked up in town. "Hello, stranger," he offered back. "Wow. You look amazing."

She took the flowers then dipped in a curtsy. "Thank you."

He followed her in, eager to steal a kiss.

All three boys were lined up in a row, staring at him. Del paused.

"Don't worry," Stacy assured him as she tucked the flowers into a vase, "They're not coming on the date with us, They wanted to say hello."

"Hey, guys." Del waved at Colt and ruffled Ace's hair. "Blaze, what's a wolf's favourite time of the year?"

Blaze's eyes sparkled. "I don't know, what?"

"The *howl*idays."

The three of them acted like he'd just headlined on Broadway, giggling with childish delight as they surrounded him and hugged him tight.

"Okay, we need to go," Stacy told her boys. "One more kiss for me, and then you be good for your aunties."

They kissed her, and Ace also kissed Del. Then they raced off up the stairs stomping like a herd of wild ponies.

Stacy took Del by the hand and led him out the back door. "And now, time for us."

They walked hand in hand across the lawn, summer heat shimmering around them. "You didn't tell me where we're going," Del reminded her.

"It's a surprise." She led him onto the dock, all the way to the end where the table sat in regal majesty. The umbrella over the table was angled just right to give the table shade while leaving them the mountain and lake view. She pulled out a chair for him. "*Surprise.*"

Del laughed, enchanted by her. "It's perfect, although I might be overdressed for this restaurant."

"You look gorgeous," she told him as he sat. Stacy leaned over the back of his chair and pressed a kiss to his cheek. "You're a handsome man, Del. I mean, handsome shifter, because your wolf is also very dashing."

A rush of heat lit his cheeks as his wolf rolled in the compliment.

She sat opposite him, and he couldn't look away. "I might have trouble eating," he warned. "You're taking my breath away."

"I hope you can eat a little. You need to keep up your

strength." Mischief danced in her eyes. She pointed to the cooler to the right of the table. "There's wine in there, if you'd do the honours."

Del found a chilled bottle of pinot gris and opened it, pouring into their two glasses. By the time he was done, Stacy had placed a small plate in front of each of them, with a third in the middle of the table.

Small portions of quiche and smoked salmon were arranged like works of art, and his mouth watered as the scent of meat and cheese hit his system. "It's nearly too pretty to eat."

Stacy picked up one of the chocolate dipped strawberries from the middle of the table. "Nearly, but I hope you can't resist taking a bite."

"I can't," he confessed. "Count on it."

Amusement danced between them. "I was talking about the food."

"Oh?" Del smiled before steering them down a different path for a while. "Tell me about your family. I want to know more."

They sat under the umbrella and discussed family, friends. Education and hobbies. He didn't want this part of the night to end as he learned about all the little things that excited her and the hopes she still had for the future. They shared a magic of an entirely different sort as Stacy continued to pull delicious plates from the trolley beside them. They chatted for hours as the sun slowly drifted across the sky toward the mountains.

When the final course was done and Stacy rose and took him by the hand, Del was contented to the core of his soul.

They strolled past the viewing bench that had starred in their shared dirty dream—man, only the night before?

Stacy's lips curled upward, and her cheeks were rosy as she walked past the spot.

"You don't want to sit and *talk* for a while?" Del teased.

"We've established now that talking is talking and fooling around is fooling around. But I do want to watch the sunset." She pointed toward the grassy slope easing toward the lake.

They sat, side by side and hand in hand, quiet now instead of chattering. The distant sound of the boys laughing carried to them, and Del smiled. This night wasn't about the kids, but each of Stacy's sons had a place in the picture. There was no escaping that truth.

It was inching past nine when Stacy lifted her head from Del's shoulder and prodded him to his feet. "Our date isn't over. Come with me."

He should be patient and wait to see what came next, but he really wanted to know. "Are you taking me home with you, sweet Stacy? Do we get another sleepover?"

"No, and yes," she added before he could be disappointed. She guided him onto the porch of the most remote cabin. "I expect we'll have plenty of future mornings where the children will be up before we want them to be. And they're still young enough I'm not ready to lock them out." Stacy cupped Del's face and met his eyes. "Tonight I want time with you. *Only* with you. The only way that's happening is not being under the same roof as them."

She pushed open the door of the cabin.

STACY HAD PUT some effort into the meal, but that had been second nature to her. She'd agonized over the room for an hour before her sister had hauled her away.

It had been a long time since Stacy had set the tone for romance. And thinking back on why wasn't for tonight. Tonight was about looking forward.

No. Tonight was about *tonight*. Being present. Being here.

With Del.

Stepping through the door, she looked around at the dozens of flickering lights. The battery-powered candles danced like fireflies, reflecting off the golden walls and the yellow quilt she'd taken from her room and spread across the queen-size mattress.

One stolen second to ensure her preparations hadn't vanished while she'd been away, then she turned her attention on Del.

Would he be looking around with that frank, assessing way he had? Would he be smiling at the charm she'd tried to instill?

All his attention was firmly fixed on her, his expression soft and gentle. "Thank you for bringing the quilt."

"You painted a vivid picture involving that quilt." Barely a whisper, need holding her so tight she could barely speak. "Del?"

"Yes, darling?"

She smiled. "Make love to me?"

Del nodded. "Absolutely. But first..."

He placed his phone on the dresser next to a set of candles. It was followed by a Bluetooth speaker. A moment later, the sweet sounds of classical guitar filled the air, along with a waterfall and other wilderness noises. A perfect blend of man-made music and nature's offering.

A moment later, he took her in his arms and twirled them, guiding her so expertly Stacy didn't have time to worry if she was about to step on his toes. "Why am I not surprised you can dance?"

"I don't just dance, I *like* to dance," he told her. The fingers of the hand at her back spread wide, pressing them closer, heating her gradually from the outside in. Her cheek brushed his, the gentle scratch of his beard growing more familiar.

They danced while the sunlight shining in the window faded to the reds and oranges of a sultry summer day. Then Del took her face in his hands and kissed her. Slow and sweet. A whispering caress that sent a shiver up her spine. Sent need flaring, hot and bright, and slow went out the window.

Stacy pushed his jacket from his shoulders, fingers eager on his buttons. He swore, clutching at his tie and jerking it back and forth to get it to loosen. Then laughter filled in the gaps as she pushed his hands away and undid the knot he'd created in his hurry. As he undid her zipper, the shoulders of her sundress were on the verge of slipping from her body.

As fabric fell away to leave her standing in her bra and undies, and him in...nothing.

Dear lord, the man was *built*.

"You're like a living, breathing Adonis statue." Stacy pressed her palm to his chest because she could. His heart pulsed beneath her fingers, and she scratched lightly, savouring the moan she brought forth.

"Living, breathing, *moving*," he added, his mouth tracing a path down the edge of her bra a second before it magically vanished. Kisses now on her skin, against the pulse point in her neck, over the tip of her nipple.

Stacy clutched his head and enjoyed the rising beat in her core.

One easy motion later, she was in the air, carried to the

bed. Lowered onto the pretty yellow quilt as if she were breakable. He crawled over her, the predator with his prey. Eyes glowing with heat as he breathed deep and smiled in satisfaction. "You're turned on. Wanting me. Wanting us."

"Yes." Stacy pulled his lips to hers and they kissed even while his hands explored, teased, stroked.

He slipped under the edge of her panties, and strong fingers brushed her curls. He traced the skin over her clit as if unearthing a priceless treasure. Then firmer, his touch, like his kiss, turning more demanding, more possessive.

Stacy gasped as he pushed inside her, fingers firm, thumb still working that sensual rhythm on her clit. "Del. I want you."

"You've got me." A nip of her lower lip. Her earlobe.

He stroked deeper and she arched into his hand. "I want more. I want your *cock*."

His lips curled against hers. "Well, now."

She couldn't help laughing with him softly, because it was fun being in bed with him. Learning how to mesh, learning how to make this right for them both. "Do you want me to talk dirty to you? Is that your thing?"

"My thing is knowing what you want, so saying you need my cock is just fine. My thing is your hands on my body, touching me," Del said. "I'll deal with the dirty talk."

A shiver rippled over her. He rose suddenly, ripped off her panties, and put his mouth on her sex. His fingers were back a second later, lighting up the places that turned her insides into a ticking time bomb of pleasure. She worked to touch the only parts of him she could reach. Feet on his back, hands in his hair. "Del. I'm so close."

"Come on my tongue. I'll take you up again," he promised.

She thrashed her head on the pillow. "No, now. Inside me, *now*."

Stubborn though he might be, the desperation in her voice was clear. Del was over her now, settling between her thighs. Cock nudging her sex as he linked their fingers and pressed her hands to the mattress on either side of her head.

Held down, held still, held *close*, Stacy savoured the feeling of power over her. She looked into Del's eyes as he rocked forward and gently joined them as one.

So good. So...

Full. Stacy's lips twitched. The man was substantial. "Give me a second or two," she whispered.

Del's grin burst out like the morning sun. "You're good for my ego. I've got it. You enjoy the ride."

He moved so slowly she wasn't sure it was happening until he clearly was no longer deep in her sex. The reverse trip took just as long and was just as torturously pleasurable. Again and again, as Stacy stared into Del's face and saw more than physical pleasure reflected there.

Harder now, a steady rhythm that sent her insides spiraling toward the edge. She wrapped her legs around him and held on with everything she had. "Del. Yes, harder."

He squeezed her hands and increased pace again.

They broke together, the small zaps in her belly dancing over her skin like teeny kisses and big booming flashes. Del groaned, dipping his head to take her lips once more. His hips pulsed helplessly as he lost control and joined the fireworks display happening right there in the bedroom.

When they ended up on the mattress, side by side, they were still tangled together. Legs and hands, heavy breathing as the air between them tangled as well.

Stacy brushed her fingers over his forehead. "I liked that."

"Me too."

A grin escaped. "I like your cock."

Del laughed, rolling her on top of him. "I like that you like my cock." He brushed a loose strand of hair back behind her ear. "Now, what time is your curfew? I need to know how soon I need to sneak you back to your rooms so I can plan how quickly we do that all over again."

"I need to be in the kitchen at eight a.m."

"*Hallelujah*," he muttered before waggling his brows in a mock evil-villain impression. "Shower now or more ravishing?"

"Ravishing in the shower?"

He nodded as if it was the most brilliant suggestion ever.

17

Stacy caught herself whistling in the kitchen and guiltily tried to stop before one of the girls said something. Again.

It had been nearly a week since the date, and since then, she and Del had continued to spend time together. With the boys and without them. They'd found times to steal away for privacy as well, and it seemed being well sexed-up made Stacy whistle. Even thinking about the sweet sexy times...

Yup, she was whistling again.

She glanced over at Sophie, and her hopes fell. The young woman was industriously cutting fresh pasta into strips on the counter, but her smirk said it all.

"Well, I can't help it," Stacy complained, sliding to Sophie's side to examine her work. "I'm happy."

"You are happy." Sophie agreed before snorting in a most unladylike way. "Oh my gosh, I'm sorry. But you were also *happy* at least a couple times this morning."

Jessica on the other side of the room made a choking sound. "Sophie. That's so rude."

"I know." Sophie was now nearly crying with laughter. "But *someone* has to tell her."

"Tell me what?" Stacy folded her arms over her chest and used her most mom look on the two of them. "Tell me what?" she demanded again.

Carrying the bowl of chicken she'd finished deboning, Jessica paced to the other side of the kitchen and popped it into the cooler before bravely marching to a spot in front of Stacy. "We're wolves. And that means..." She glanced at Sophie as if asking for help.

Sophie motioned frantically for her to continue.

Jessica dipped her chin, met Stacy's eyes, and let it rip. "Scents are strong, you know. Some stronger than others. Like every time you spot Del out the window, we know because your scent changes."

Sophie leaned over Jessica's shoulder as if gaining strength from her safe hiding spot. "And we really know when you two have sex. Like, you must be exhausted from all the orgasms and—"

Stacy's hand shot up involuntarily as her cheeks heated to boiling. "Stop right there. I know I asked, but let's not finish this particular conversation, okay?"

"Wolves always know," Sophie said, still smiling brightly. "We're not usually rude enough to say anything. But you're so cute, I couldn't help myself."

It appeared asking wolves for blunt information was never a good idea. "I'm not mad and not really embarrassed. Well, not too embarrassed." She met Jessica's gaze. "Okay, I'm totally embarrassed, but I'm also happily sexed-up, so it's a win in the end."

"Always." Jessica's grin blazed cheerfully.

Stacy took a deep breath. "Well, you guys know that I'm still learning, so thank you for the heads-up. And if I am missing or messing up some other vital information about wolves in the future, I need you to tell me, okay? Promise?"

The young ladies were side by side now, watching her intently. "You sure?" Sophie asked.

"I'm sure. We've come a long way in a short time, and I trust you two completely."

They both bloomed like crocuses in the spring, happiness unfurling right before Stacy's eyes.

Except Jessica's joy lasted for only a second before it vanished. Erased as if a hand had swiped across her face and left nothing but terror behind.

She pressed a hand to her mouth then whirled and raced from the room.

Stacy and Sophie stood there in shock.

"Did I—" Stacy began.

Sophie shook her head, running for the door. "It's nothing to do with what we were talking about. Let me go see what's wrong."

Outside on the back porch, Stacy watched the conversation happening down by the water's edge where Jessica had retreated to. Sophie held one of Jessica's hands and was speaking earnestly to the other woman.

"Problems in the kitchen?" Marvin sauntered up beside her, folding his arms as he gazed toward the lake. Daisy happily bounced a ball a few feet away. She paused to wave at Stacy before continuing to sing and bounce.

"Nothing bad," Stacy offered cautiously, even though she was still clueless. She glanced beside her. "Where are the boys?"

He pointed to the far side of the lake where three canoes were preparing to head out onto the mirror-like surface. "The guys took them. Daisy didn't want to go on the water, and I'm more of a swimmer than a paddler."

"Swim or wade?"

Marvin winked, then pretended to doggie paddle.

His gaze turned again to Stacy's assistant chefs. "They've nearly got it straightened out."

"You can tell from here?" Stacy was tempted to ask if he also knew what the problem was but decided to wait out of respect for Jessica's privacy.

"Sure. It's all in the body language." He took a deep breath and eyed her. "You're settling in with the pack, ain'tcha?"

"Appears I am."

"Good. They need your touch. You understand that power isn't all about *power*." Marvin motioned to Sophie, who now had her arm around a crying Jessica. "The quiet ones. The ones with soft power can break down mountains."

"Like water over rocks, slowly carving it away?"

"Or sometimes not so slowly." Marvin shrugged. "This pack is learning, though, so I'm happy. It's not always easy being the smartest shifter in the territory, but I have high hopes this group will eventually get it right."

"With your help, I'm sure they will," she offered brightly.

He snickered. "See, there you go, being all watery and sweet and making me mind my p's and q's because you're just about the cutest thing I've ever seen."

Relief slipped in as she spotted Jessica and Sophie returning to the lodge. Jessica was no longer crying but held her head high.

"*Just* about the cutest thing? I'm disappointed." Stacy batted her lashes at Marvin.

A burst of laughter escaped him. "You stop flirting.

You're already spoken for, and I've got my eye on someone, so we're both taken."

Oh, now this was interesting. "Tell me who you're sweet on. I won't share," she promised.

Daisy ran up and held her ball out to him. "Come play," she demanded before thinking hard and adding, "please."

"Of course, sugar." Marvin accepted the ball then lifted a brow at Stacy, tilting his head toward the young ladies. "You're needed over there."

Stacy was already walking that direction, but she called out one final teasing warning. "I will figure it out, Marvin. Just you wait."

Inside the kitchen, Jessica was drying her face, and Sophie was back to work on her pasta. Entering quietly, Stacy made her way to Jessica's side.

The other woman straightened. "I'm okay. Sophie helped, and you didn't do anything wrong. But you need to know that I'm so grateful for getting to work here, and I will *never* do anything to break your trust." Her voice was wavering again, control slipping.

Stacy caught her in a tight hug. "I'm glad to hear it."

Jessica hugged her fiercely before pushing back, determination written all over her. "Also, I have a favour to ask. If it's okay, can I stay in one of the cabins here for the next few days? They're doing something with the plumbing at my place, and I don't want to live without water."

"Of course, you can," Stacy assured her. "Let me go grab you a key to one of the cabins."

She patted the woman's shoulder before going to retrieve a key for her.

Power moves. Huh. She was learning new wolf tricks every day.

STANDING at the edge of the lake with three canoes, Jace, Blue, and the boys, Del breathed deep in anticipation of a great afternoon.

"I want to paddle with Del."

Three voices rang out at the same time, and as amazing as his ego felt at that, Del went into instant solution mode. "But I want to paddle with Jace."

Jace snickered. "Yeah, that's not happening."

"Well, you need help, dude." Del turned to face the boys then lowered his voice. "Jace can't steer very well. He might get stuck in the middle of the lake without a really good paddler helping him."

"Colt's the bestest paddler," Ace whispered back so loudly they probably heard him in the lodge.

"Favour to ask," Del said to Colt, tilting his head toward Jace.

Colt knew what was going on, but he winked where his brothers couldn't see then waved at Jace. "Hey, can I be your partner?"

"Delighted." Jace pointed to the red canoe. "That one's ours. Come on."

"Look, there's a rainbow canoe," Ace shouted.

"I want to ride in the rainbow canoe," Blaze shouted even louder.

"That's mine," Blue said dryly, eyeing Del. "Damn, you're good."

"Hey, Mr. Blue." Blaze rushed over to his side. "You said damn. You know what you call a wolf who uses bad language?"

Blue grabbed the paddles and handed one to Blaze. "Nope."

"A swear-wolf." Blaze had the bow of the canoe in the water before Blue had finished rolling his eyes.

Ace tugged on Del's shorts until he picked the kid up. "I get to paddle with you," Ace announced in a very self-satisfied tone.

"You do. You're a smarty-pants for knowing Blaze likes rainbows." Del winked at Ace.

They were barely out on the water before the little tyke grabbed the gunwales of the canoe and twisted to face the second canoe. "Hey, Blue, why did the wolf cross the road?"

"Wait, no. *I* tell the wolf jokes," Blaze complained. He lifted his paddle and smacked it down, sending a wave of water flying everywhere, including all over himself and Blue. "Oops?"

"Del told a wolf joke the other day," Colt pointed out.

Blaze wrinkled his nose. "He did. It was a one good, too."

"Maybe we should *all* tell one wolf joke today," Blue suggested. "Okay?"

After a little consideration, Blaze nodded. "Okay."

"Good, because if I tell a wolf pun, it will be *howl*arious." Blue held up his arms in a muscleman pose then leaned forward as if taking a bow.

Three pairs of little boy eyes stared at him in confusion.

Blue tried again. "*Hoooowl*arious. Get it?"

Blaze sniffed, obviously disappointed but not wanting to hurt Blue's feelings. "It was really good, Mr. Blue. Mr. Jace, your turn."

The canoes were side-by-side now, gliding forward toward the point of land in front of the lodge. Jace cleared his throat. "What's my favourite green vegetable?"

"Is this a wolf joke?" Blue demanded, out of sorts from his joke failing.

"I'm a wolf, aren't I?" Jace winked at Blaze. "Know what I love? *Aroooo*-gula."

Snickers all around. Colt shot up a hand. "My turn. Blaze and Ace, knock, knock!"

"Who's there?" his brothers shouted in reply.

Colt's eyes sparkled as he met Del's gaze. "*Howl.*"

"*Howl*, who?"

"*Howl* you know unless you open the door?"

Blaze patted his belly as he guffawed, and Ace bounced up and down hard enough that Del had to paddle to keep them balanced.

"Ace, finish your joke. Why did the wolf cross the road?" Del prompted.

"He was chasing the chicken." Ace laughed at his own joke as he leapt up and turned around, paddle ignored as he concentrated on the jokes more than the canoe trip. "Your turn, Mr. Del."

"I guess I'd better make it a good one. Let's see..." Del aimed their canoe farther away from the rainbow one, but Blaze seemed determined to paddle them with gunwales nearly touching. "Which animal is grey, has four legs, howls at the moon...and eats cement?"

Ace opened his mouth then frowned at the final part of the question. "It's a wolf, but they don't eat cement."

Jace was already snickering. "Oh, I get it. It is a wolf, Ace. Del threw in the cement *to make it hard.*"

Groans and laughter this time. Blue dipped his paddle to splash water at Del, only Blaze decided to do the same thing at the same time, and their canoe tipped instantly.

As if watching a slow-motion reel, Del saw the rest of the disaster in minute detail. Blue grabbed for Blaze, who grabbed for the nearest upright object. Which meant the full weight of the two landed on the side of Del's canoe. He attempted to shift his weight in the other direction, falling over the side into Jace's canoe, which instantly tipped.

Seconds later, five heads bobbed above the water as Del frantically looked for the sixth.

The only one still in an upright canoe, Ace's head rose over the edge of the gunwale, his eyes wide as he examined the chaos around him. "Are we going swimming or canoeing?"

"A little of both," Jace offered.

"Wait for me." The kid cannonballed over the edge, nearly taking Del out. Ace popped up like a cock, his lifejacket holding his head high above the water. "Okay. I'm ready."

Blaze clung to the end of one canoe, a determined expression on his little face. "Last joke. What's the first thing a wolf does when he falls in the lake?"

"No idea," Blue said, tossing random floating items into the lone upright canoe. "What's the first thing he does?"

"He gets wet," Blaze announced with a chuckle. "Sorry, everybody."

"It's okay. We're wash-and-wear wolves, remember?" Del winked at him. "Change of plans. Next lesson—how to recover from a tipping incident."

Much splashing and laughter followed, and while it wasn't the adventure they'd planned, it was still an adventure. Del took another deep breath and soaked it all in.

18

———

"Stephanie, you're a goddess."

The dining space had been transformed. Stacy stood in the open doorway, hands pressed to her cheeks, and soaked it in.

Del didn't know which way to look. At the amazing set up or how delighted Stacy was at the transformation.

For the inaugural Timberwolf Lodge Chef's Table event, they'd decided to make things easier for Stacy to cook and still witness how her creations were going over. Instead of cutting her and her assistants off from the dining room, they'd pushed open the sliding doors between the kitchen space and what could be a formal ballroom. The wooden-beamed roof towered overhead, and the long line of windows that faced the lake were all edged with twinkling LEDs.

A long farmhouse-style table stretched the entire length of the space with eight chairs on either side. The group tonight would dine family-style for some courses, plated for others, and through it all, Stacy, Sophie, and Jessica could peek around the corner and enjoy.

Blue had offered to take charge of the boys for the evening, and they were currently having a hotdog roast by their treehouse. Here at the lodge, Del was looking forward to a wonderful meal with good packmates. He was hopeful that after the meal Stacy might agree to steal away with him for a couple of nights for an extended *date your mate and maybe tell him you love him* getaway. She'd been so busy preparing for tonight she deserved a chance to get away and relax.

An hour later it was clear that while a few bugs needed to be worked out, like more staff to help with serving, the food was spot on.

Everyone lucky enough to have been invited to share the meal split their time between moaning at the flavours or *oohing* and *aahing* over the pretty presentations.

Angie was there, plus two other single ladies from the pack. Four older couples had been delighted to join them, pack members who Sophie suggested had the word-of-mouth ability to get people on board for future events. Jace, Cassidy, Stephanie, and Marvin rounded out the table.

And himself, pride pulling his shoulders back as the evening continued and the culinary genius of his mate became clearer.

They'd finished the main meal and the extra help were clearing away the plates. Stacy stood beside the table, Angie offering her exuberant praises.

"Honey, you cook like that on a regular basis, and we'll have people flying from all parts of the country to get a seat at the table," Angie said.

"Agreed." Mr. Holmes beamed at her. "I've never had better pork, and trust me, I've done some sampling in my day." He patted his large belly and chuckled with the pack members around him.

Behind him, the front door opened, slamming into the wall like usual.

Del didn't jump, knowing Blue was due back anytime with the boys, but Cassidy and others all levitated a few feet.

Cassidy pressed her lips together. Her usual cry of 'were you born in barn?' or something similar was not the right choice for this moment.

"We need to do something to that door," she informed Jace primly. "Like the opposite of greasing it. Something to make it *not* open so easily."

Clara Holmes laughed before her eyes widened and she pointed to the foyer. "Oh my. Either Emma's very late, or you have an uninvited guest."

Emma?

Del was on his feet in an instant, darting forward until he stood between the woman and the table. The usually beautiful blonde looked tattered and unkempt, her expensive clothing in shreds. For a second he worried that she'd been in an accident.

Then he smelled it. The scent, pungent and pure, not faded or in minute traces. The drug that had been his father's downfall. The drug they'd been trying to find for weeks. Emma reeked of it.

It was best to try to keep this situation as controlled as possible. There was no telling how she'd react if he simply rushed her. "Not invited is the right answer. What are you doing here, Emma?"

Her eyes flashed with anger, only this time she glared toward the kitchen where Jessica and Sophie stood. "*You.* What have you done?"

"What was right," Jessica said in a whisper.

"You should have done as you were told," Emma

screamed in frustration, stepping menacingly toward Jessica.

Sophie slipped between them at the same moment Del adjusted his position. Out of lunging range, close enough he could attack if needed.

Sorrow filled him. Regret, along with a wave of memories. He hoped the same solution wasn't needed again.

"It's okay, I got this," Jessica said louder. She squeezed Sophie's shoulder then snuck past her, chin still high, fear held in check. "I decided to do what was best for my pack, and you aren't it."

"You will regret this. I will ruin you." Spittle flew as Emma roared the words.

Jessica turned to face Stacy. "Emma wants control of the pack. She has proof that I cheated during some tests I took years ago, so my certificate isn't real. She made me get the job here so that I could slip something into the food tonight. She planned to show up after all of you got sick so she could do as she pleased, but I didn't do it." Her chin higher still, she darted a disgusted gaze Emma's direction before returning to Stacy. "I don't care if I lose my certificate. You trusted me, and you *can* trust me."

"You're dead. As soon as I'm in charge, you're all *dead*," Emma growled, hands shifting back and forth from fingers to claws as if she wasn't in control of her own body.

Del stepped closer, forcing her attention on him. "Interesting sentiment, but since you're here and have clearly issued a challenge, we'll go ahead and do this the old-fashioned way."

"Get out of my way, Del," Emma sneered. "You're weak. You gave up being Alpha. You're *weak* and *useless*, and not worth spitting on."

Gee, that assessment could give a guy a complex if he gave a rat's ass what the woman thought.

"You want to challenge for leadership?" Jace still hadn't moved from lounging lazily in his chair, an obvious statement that Emma wasn't worth his effort. He drawled the question as if it was the most incomprehensible thing he'd ever heard. "Both Cassidy and I can kick your ass. I don't see this going well for you."

"Of course not you. Or her," Emma darted an angry glare at Cassidy.

"Remind me sometime to tell you all about how Cassidy put the hurt on little Emma here the first time they met." Stephanie curled one lip and sniffed as if Emma had tracked in something ripe.

"Don't be so modest," Cassidy offered. "You were the one who hogtied her."

"Really?" Mrs. Holmes sat up, curiosity all over her. "That sounds—"

"Shut up. Shut up all of you," Emma screamed again before her head swung to where Stacy stood. "I challenge *her*. The new one who thinks she's so smart. So able to control the mangy little puppies of this pack. I don't care how you've bewitched them, I will end you."

"Stacy is not open to be challenged." Jace still drawled the comment as if they were discussing if dessert should be served now or after a walk.

"Please, she stinks like him." Emma pointed at Del. "Fated mates, are you? Waiting for the right romantic moment to tell your human? Screw that. Or, should I say, you did *screw that*. You're as good as mated, which makes her leadership, and I challenge her."

This was not happening. "No." Del repeated Jace's response. "You want a piece of the Enforcer, that's me."

The front door remained open behind Emma, and suddenly Stacy's three boys rushed in, laughter and roaring noises vanishing as they jerked to a stop inches from the unwanted guest.

Blue bounced in behind them, surprise flashing into his eyes.

Before anyone else could move, Emma darted back, hand swinging toward the children.

Shouts rang out loud. Growls. Colt shifted instantly, teeth bared as he tried to get between her and his brothers. Blaze tripped over Colt and fell to the ground.

Which left Ace, his gaze darting across the room to Stacy as Emma snatched him up. "Mama?"

Emma leapt away, holding him in front of her like a shield. "You want to try that refusal again? Or are you ready to fight?"

Fear, bone deep and cold, cut across Stacy's face, then she spoke with power and conviction. "Let. Him. Go."

Everyone in the room felt the power in her words.

Emma wavered on her feet. Her frown deepened. "What... *What* did you say?"

It appeared mama bear mode had been activated.

Stacy stepped around the table, and that's when Del noticed she was carrying a very large knife.

Nothing but anger remained. For one instant, Stacy had been paralyzed with fear, the sight of her little boy in this wild woman's clutches sickening and soul-numbing.

The next second, rage had risen. Yet she somehow walked calmly to the space beside Del, the heat inside her no less intense, but a molten fury she contained within a layer of icy stillness.

"Stacy, be careful," Del warned. "Emma's taken the same drug my dad got into."

Her insides curled. Another layer of deception and betrayal. To inflict that memory, that hurt, on such a good man was beyond forgiveness.

Stacy's mind danced with a tangle of words and ideas. Marvin's comments about power— The quiet power of the soft touch. The changes made to the pack in a soft and gentle way. Like a mother finding the right handle to steer their children. Some needed humour, some needed rules, but they all needed love.

Stacy considered all of that as she met Ace's gaze across the space. He fought valiantly to keep from crying. Her innocent little boy who was nothing but heart and happiness, scared because this woman wanted to... Not to lead, but to be an all-powerful overlord.

This woman, who had taken the same drug that Del had needed to kill his father over.

The truth hit hard and pure. Yes, maybe everyone had a different handle that could be turned to make changes. But sometimes the discipline that a mom offered was tough love. Exactly what needed to be handed out to maybe, just maybe, make a change for a better future.

Blue had cleared her other children from the danger zone. Stacy stood beside Del with only Emma and Ace in front of her, the pack and her friends at her back.

She laid her left hand on Del's arm. "My job," she said quietly.

A tremble shook him hard. His desire to protect nearly overpowered him before trust and love snapped into place like a tangible thing.

He took a step back and left her alone.

Never alone. I'm always here.

The words were there in her mind. His wolf, reassuring her, loving her.

Stacy pushed a mental kiss back through their connection then focused on Emma. "Put my son down, then you and I will have our discussion."

She expected Emma to outright refuse or to toss Ace away and lunge for her. Both of those made sense in a nonsensical kind of way. Another round of boasting or a straight-up attack. Stacy was leaning toward Emma's need to gloat a little more, to monologue like in some bad streaming movie with B-grade actors.

Sure enough, ego won. Emma adjusted her grip on Ace, clutching him with her left arm so she could raise the clawed fingers of her right in a menacing wave. "So the mouse wants to play with the wolf. How sweet. You know, it's disappointing you didn't all end up drowning that very first day. It would have been so much easier."

"Accidents happen." Stacy was proud her voice didn't waver even as the memory of being trapped by the river rushed in. The fear she'd lost Colt forever, the panic of not being able to save her sons.

The cool, calm reassurance of Del as he'd done what was needed.

From that first moment, he'd been there.

Emma threw back her head and howled, a crackling laugh mixing in that turned it into a nightmare soundtrack. "An accident?" She sneered at Stacy. "*I* sent you the directions. The only mistake I made was not being sure the bridge was ready to go quicker."

The fire inside Stacy flared even brighter. "*You* sent the map?"

The map that had nearly gotten them all killed.

"I've sent lots of messages lately," Emma gloated. She shook Ace lightly. "You should have kept your babies safe, Mama. You should have stayed away from Timberwolf Lodge, so full of dangerous wolves."

Stacy had heard enough. She looked Ace in the eyes and smiled. "Wolves are not the only ones with teeth who can bite. And bite hard."

It happened faster than expected, but then again, Stacy had raised smart babies. Even as Stacy rushed forward, Emma screamed, twisting from where Ace had sunk his little teeth into her biceps. She ripped him off her, and Ace flew.

Del was there, scooping him up before he hit the floor, retreating out of Stacy's peripheral vision. Good, she had other matters to focus on.

Like ducking under the clawed hand sweeping past her face and twisting to grab hold of Emma from behind. Stacy dug her fingers into the fresh bite mark her son had left on the woman's upper arm, adjusted her stance, and took control.

The carving knife in her right hand balanced delicately at Emma's throat.

Emma stilled. "You wouldn't."

"Take a sniff," Stacy suggested. "Do I smell afraid? Do I smell as if I don't know how to do what needs to be done?"

Everyone in the room seemed to take a deep inhale, which would have been hugely amusing if it wasn't happening right now, in this way.

"Go ahead," Emma taunted. "Kill me."

"Where's the fun in that?" Stacy taunted back. "Did you know that they now use pig cadavers in biology class for the dissections?"

Emma stayed silent, her feet wiggling the slightest bit as if trying to get a better stance. Stacy pressed the knife a little harder to her neck, and a thin line of blood oozed from the small cut she'd made.

"Pigs have a nearly perfect match to the human anatomical structure, and while I know you're a shifter, right now you're in your human form." Stacy hummed happily. "We had pork for dinner. Did you know I can break down an entire pig in under twenty minutes? You see where I'm going with this?"

"What do you want?" Emma muttered.

"For you to leave Timberwolf Lodge. I don't know the specific wolf shifter rules, but I'm pretty sure there has to be something on the books that means you get gone, and you never, *ever* come near my family again. Or I will be setting a timer and trying for a new record."

The woman in her arms tensed. The sick scent, like skunk, hung on the air, and for a split second Stacy wondered. No matter how tempting her offer was, would the drug force Emma to choose poorly?

The human under her knife melted into a wolf, fur slipping through Stacy's fingers. She jerked the blade out and away, not wanting to accidentally slit Emma's throat.

Without a backward glance, Emma darted through the open door.

Del and Jace were after her instantly, their nails scratching at the hardwood floors as two dark wolves shot out the foyer. Stacy dropped the knife to the floor then rushed forward, the pack and her friends at her back. As they filled the porch area, she spotted Blue joining the chase.

Satisfied Emma was being taken care of, Stacy searched frantically for her children.

Blaze popped up from behind a bush across the parking lot. "Blue said to hide until it was safe," he shouted. Colt appeared at his feet, still in wolf form. "Is it safe?"

"Yes, come home." Stacy gave a feverish wave, whirling to find the last of them.

"Here's your baby." Stephanie handed Ace over. "I'll grab the other two."

Stacy squeezed Ace as hard as she dared. "You were so brave."

"I bit her," Ace confessed. "I'm sorry. I promised to never bite anyone again, but I did."

"You were perfect, and you did exactly what I told you to. I think the rules are different now than in your old daycare," Stacy said, tapping him on the nose and smiling. "Little wolves sometimes need to use their teeth."

He bared them at her then burst out crying, burying his face against her neck.

She held him and let him weep as she knelt to accept Blaze and Colt into the embrace. Her sons, her heart, safe.

Del. The missing part of the unit. Because there was no use in pretending anymore that she needed time, or that humans simply didn't do things like fall in love in mere days.

This human had, and Del needed to know that.

19

They chased Emma to the edge of Jasper territory, three powerful wolves all holding themselves back just a little. At any point they could have overtaken her and removed the threat once and for all.

But Stacy had asked for Emma to be banished—

Not that she'd known the right words to ask for it, but they all knew. Del, Jace, and Blue knew that if there had been a wolf manual, Stacy would have pointed to this option.

As they topped the pass that was the far eastern border, all three of them stopped, shifted, and stared at the single female who shifted barely twenty feet from them. The thin line on her neck still bled.

Jace pulled himself upright, the mantle of Alpha surrounding him as clearly as if he'd pulled on a robe. "Emma Wilson, you are no longer a member of this pack. You are not welcome on these lands where our wolves roam, nor in the human places. All this territory is forbidden to you, and the pack will be told. Show up unannounced, and you die."

She bared her teeth, her growl more animal than human.

"One Enforcer of the pack has already told you her demands." Del said it softly, but pride rang in his voice. "So I'll just add that while Stacy can render a pig in twenty minutes, my wolf can do it in ten."

Her gaze flickered for a single moment, then she turned to face Blue. "Going to threaten me, too, Omega? Or are you only capable of hurting people with your stupid clothing choices?"

Power sang on the ridge, a sharp tingling sensation that lifted Del's hair. Light flashed, and a second later, Emma was on her butt on the ground.

She blinked hard, expression full of horror as she stared at Blue. "How…"

"It's never good to attack someone when you don't know what caliber they're carrying." Blue's tone went gentle as if he were sad. "Go away, Emma. Find somewhere to lick your wounds and get the drug out of your system. I'll tell your family you'll be in touch when you're feeling more…yourself."

She shifted and loped off, her stride uneven. They watched until she disappeared into the shadows of the trees.

Jace turned. "That was…" He stepped in front of Blue, shaking his head. "What *was* that?"

"Our Omega's been keeping secrets." Del eyed his cousin. "Since I see no pockets that might hold random remotes for a satellite link, want to tell us how you did that?"

"It's new," Blue told them. "I think Stephanie did something to me."

"You wish she did something to you," Jace teased as they headed back to the lodge.

"That too," Blue agreed, "but my powers of woohoo are out of kilter these days. I am so fucking sorry I walked the boys straight into Emma. I should have known. I usually *would* have known. I'm no longer seeing glimpses of the future the same way."

"You lost *precognition*, but got *lightning bolt* in exchange?" Del shook his head. "There's got to be a reason. But don't beat yourself up. None of us knew Emma was behind this, and I spent three weeks sniffing all over town. I should have found some clue."

"Thank God Jessica didn't poison us all." Jace tilted his chin at Del. "Stacy's work. She's got the heart of the pack right there in her palm, and it saved our butts this time."

"She's got my heart there, too," Del said softly. "I need to get back."

They shifted, ran. A different kind of urgency carried Del's feet forward. The need to be there, the need to be with his pack, his family. His mate.

It was as if a thread between them had been stretched too thin, and with every step closer to Timberwolf Lodge, he became a little more whole. More contented.

More...Delaney Vezina.

Not Alpha or pack Enforcer. Not a lawyer, or businessman, or any of those titles he'd worked so hard to achieve. He was simply a shifter who had a mate who loved him—

Dear God, he hoped that was true.

They made it back to the lodge, and he was shifting even as his paws hit the porch stairs.

"Del."

Stacy stood beside the chairs they'd sat in only a couple weeks ago to discuss dating. He headed to her side and tucked her against his body.

She clung tightly, kissing his face, petting him all over until he finally took a gasp of air. He'd been too busy making sure she was okay to even breathe.

He stared into her eyes. "The boys. Ace. How are they?"

She laughed softly, then handed him a pair of sweatpants to pull on. "They're good. They're probably still in the kitchen eating way too much dessert. And they want to see you, but I told them I got to see my mate first. That we needed to deal with some things for the pack, and you needed to find some clothes because we're not all wolves around here, but that we would tuck them into bed tonight. Together."

"Good. That's good." He froze, one foot in the pants, one foot still out, her words jumbling through his brain. "Your...*mate*?"

She pressed her palm to his face. "It's pretty clear that I made some choices today. I *chose* to be pack Enforcer. I *chose* to use my skills as I thought best, and you backed my play."

"You were..." He shivered for a second then hurriedly finished dressing. "You are so fucking hot when you're a badass."

Stacy laughed, touching her forehead to his. "I like being a badass. But I also think I'm ready to *choose* to be your mate. If that's okay."

"So okay," he agreed. He whirled her in a circle, happiness bubbling up from deep inside. When he put her feet back on the ground, he kissed her gently. Just a promise of what was to come. "I'm glad you and the boys are safe. I'll tell you later all about what happened after you banished Emma. But I need to see the boys."

They walked inside the lodge and were reunited with

some of the Timberwolf Lodge people, including Jessica, who hovered by the door.

She turned toward them, gaze meeting Del's even though her shoulders drooped. "I already told Stacy this, but I'm so sorry."

"Doesn't seem as if you have much to apologize for," Del commented softly. "You were in a tough spot, but you made the right decision in the end."

Jessica snorted. "That's what Stacy said. I appreciate it, and I'm going to keep making good decisions. So it's all out there, and I can start with a clean slate—I put the note in Stacy's drawer because Emma made me. Also, I lied about not having water in my apartment. I had to stay away from Emma, so she didn't realize I'd finally decided to ignore her orders."

Del nodded.

"Jessica shared that Emma's been dirt-talking with pack on the sly. Which is probably where the WMA issues came from, and some of the over-the-top teenager angst." Stacy placed a hand on Jessica's arm. "Now that's all in the past. You did what was right when it counted."

Jessica's eyes were glassy with tears. "From now on I do what's right all the time."

"Good choice." Del added the weight of his wolf's approval to the words, and Jessica took a deep breath and relaxed before their eyes. "You're a part of Timberwolf Lodge now. We're glad."

The spontaneous hug Jessica offered nearly knocked him off his feet. Del was still chuckling softly as Jessica squeezed Stacy just as firmly, then left, head held high.

Cassidy broke away from Jace's side and stepped in front of them. "Del. Thank you."

"I didn't do anything."

She tilted her head toward Stacy. "You did one of the hardest things. You stepped back and let her do her job."

"She was pretty much taking names and kicking butt. I had fun watching," Del teased softly, his fingers still linked with his mate's.

"To catch you up, the rest of our guests went home, super enthusiastic about Timberwolf Lodge, and even more pleased by the leadership of the pack." Cassidy walked them to the kitchen. "I assume this is who you were looking for?"

They stepped in the door and were stampeded by small boys with pumpkin pie on their fingers and lips. Del knew because he got sticky kisses from both Blaze and Ace, and a tight hug from Colt.

"Everything good?" Stephanie asked from the far side of the kitchen table. She held a big mug of tea and wore a contented expression.

Del looked around the room. At his mate, his boys. At the men he was now good friends with once again. Strong women, like Steph and Cassidy, to grow the pack in the right directions—not just powerhouses but powerful connections.

He dipped his chin and nodded. "Couldn't be better."

❧

UPSTAIRS IN THEIR SUITE, Stacy had everything she wanted. Three little boys, scrubbed clean yet already slightly smelly—how did boys *do* that?

A man—her man—sitting on the bed, book in hand as he read out loud to them using voices for all the characters. Del was clearly having a blast, with Colt draped over his shoulder, Blaze tucked against his side like glue, and Ace in his lap.

The book was barely finished when Blaze sang out, "Mr. Del, what do little wolves read before bed?"

Del looked him in the eye. "Furry tales."

The boys all howled.

Del met Stacy's eyes across the room. "You guys know that your mom and I are mates, yes? Remember we told you that?"

"But you're dating." Ace dipped his chin. "And we can't come with you."

Amusement rose. "Well, not always," Stacy agreed.

"But my point is," Del said, "since your mom and I are mates, you don't need to call me Mr. Del anymore."

Surprise brightened their eyes even as the truth lit up something inside Stacy as well. She hadn't thought of this part yet.

Del obviously had, and he kept eye contact with her as he continued. "I know what I'd like you to call me, but it's got to work for you and your mom. You got any ideas?"

"You can't be uncle, because uncle means the person Auntie Steph loves." Blaze frowned then his face lit up. "Hey, you know what? We call Auntie Cassidy, auntie, so that means we can call Mr. Jace uncle now. Cool."

"Very cool," Stacy agreed. She smiled at Del. "I think maybe we should hear what you'd like. Because I can think of a bunch of variations, but it should be one that makes you happy too."

"I know the answer," Colt said softly. "If you don't mind, I think Blaze should call you dad. Or daddy, but that's a good name for Ace to use."

Ace's jaw hung open. "I've never had a daddy," he whispered with awe.

"I can have a dad? Or a daddy?" Blaze wrinkled his nose. "No, you can have daddy, Ace. I like dad better."

"Okay." Ace scrambled to his bed and held out his arms. "I'm ready for you to tuck me in, Daddy." He nodded at Colt. "I like it."

"Me, too." Del's voice held incredible happiness. "Colt? What about you, bud?"

Her oldest smiled. "I like dad as well, but I also like knowing you'll be our *father* and not just a mentor."

"Never just your mentor," Del agreed, pressing a kiss to Colt's forehead. "I've always hoped to become your father."

It took a while, but eventually goodnights were said, and then they were across the common family room and slipping into her bedroom.

Their bedroom. Stacy paused in the doorway as that truth hit as well.

Del pressed against her back, leaning down to kiss her shoulder. "Everything okay?"

She turned in his arms and smiled up sweetly. "Everything is perfect." She reached past him and locked the door. Winked. "We'll unlock it in a little while."

"Not too little of a while," Del whispered as he scooped her up in his arms.

Making love again, after all they'd experienced, was different. Richer, even though she'd known he cared for her. Wanted her. He trusted her and trusted her abilities...

The thought sent a shiver up her spine. Or maybe that was his tongue doing wicked and wonderful things to her breasts.

They were together, joined and the heat of passion rising hard and fast when Del whispered against her skin. "Ready to be mates? Are you certain?"

"Yes. And I already know it involves teeth." She sucked

in a deep breath as he slipped his hand over her clit and rubbed. "Oh, Del. Do it."

He laughed. "You've already got my cock."

There was more laughter and joy, and when he finally put his teeth to her shoulder and nipped, hard, the swell of pleasure that started in her core flooded her system until the room was full of lights and music. An entire orchestra of endorphins and sensual satisfaction.

Del groaned, called out her name, then buried himself deep in her body. She held him, stroking her hands over his firm shoulders, touching him the way he liked as he murmured how much he loved her. How much he cared for her and the boys, and how he'd always be there—

Stacy gasped.

He pulled back, alarmed. "What is it? Are you okay? Did you hear the boys?"

She shook her head, the tingle in her shoulder pulsing in time with her heart. "I never said it."

"Said what?" Del curled on his side, their hips still in contact.

She was so silly. "I can't believe it. I mean, I know you know it, but I need to say it." She sat upright, ignoring her nudity. She was mated to a wolf, and some humans just needed to get over their hang-ups. "Delaney Vezina. I. Love. You."

His smile lit up the room, and he sat there opposite her, grinning from ear to ear. "Well, that's convenient, considering we're mates and all. And we'll be raising a family, so the fact that I love the boys is also convenient."

His amusement kept growing, but she wasn't done. "I said it. Now it's your turn."

Del blinked. "Haven't I said it yet? I could have sworn that—"

Stacy pounced on him. Straight-up wolfish pouncing at its finest.

Once she had him pinned under her, straddling his torso, she folded her arms over her chest. "You seem to have missed your cue."

He outright admired her naked breasts. "Trust me, darling, I'm not missing much from this position."

Stacy snickered. "You're bad."

"I'm the big bad wolf, coming to eat you up," he warned.

She leaned over and kissed him, rubbing herself over him and driving him wild. "No *talking time* until you say it, Mr. Del."

His gaze softened, amusement slipping away. "Not Mr.. Not to the boys, never to you. Call me darling, or sweetheart, or honey, or sugar. But what I'd like most of all is for you to call me *love*.

Her throat tightened, and she pressed a hand to his lips.

"Because that's what we've got between us. I love you, Stacy. I'm so glad you took a gamble on me." He traced his fingers over the mark he'd left on her neck. "My love, my mate. Mine."

20

The end of September had arrived. Blue rocked on the porch swing, stared at the distant mountains, and avoided deep thoughts. Some days were for plotting, some for acting, and some for being still and listening. That's what his mentor had once told him.

Blue knew his path as a wolf was far different from Jace's or Del's. It pretty much meant that when something poked him, hard, he needed to go back to the beginning and do what he'd been taught was best for an Omega wolf.

Sit and listen it was.

The breeze on the air held hints of ice carried to Timberwolf Lodge all the way from the glaciers on the far side of the mountains. Winter was coming. Time was passing.

Stephanie still wasn't his...

He groaned, closed his eyes, and slouched. "Not what I want to listen to," he complained.

"You have an ear bud in the other ear?" The swing rocked as someone joined him. "Because I don't hear anything."

Blue's eyes snapped open as he straightened and whipped his head to the right. "How did you sneak up on me like that?" he complained, shocked that his wolf allowed anyone to tiptoe up on him like that.

Then again, it was Steph. His wolf was totally gone over her already.

She lifted a hand in front of his face and shimmied her fingers. "Maybe I'm magic."

She *was* magic. Had magically knocked his feet from under him in all the right ways. Even as he bantered with her for the next while, Blue struggled between a *this is good* and *this sucks* sensation.

When Stephanie rested her head on his shoulder, for a split second, something sizzled up Blue's skin to the back of his neck. It was gone before he could truly analyze it. Steph didn't seem to notice.

So he tilted his head enough that they connected gently, touching each other now from hip to head as they stared at the mountains.

Connected...but not yet.

It would happen when it was supposed to. *They* would happen. He was sure of it.

Dear God, just don't make him wait too much longer or he was going to turn into a bundle of furry frustration. Not a good place for an Omega wolf to hang out. He'd end up making the entire pack jittery.

But here and now, Blue took the small bit of affection Stephanie was comfortable giving him and savoured it.

He nudged her lightly with his elbow. "This is nice."

"Yeah," she said, her long, slow breaths matching time with his. "It is."

They grinned at each other.

Blue stared into her eyes. Sometimes he thought he

should win a prize for being patient beyond belief. And then she'd look at him with those big bright blue eyes, and he knew he'd wait forever if that's what it took.

She winked. "It's so nice and peaceful, it means something is bound to come along any second now and blow it all up."

"Oh, you bright and shining optimist."

"Ain't I just?" she agreed.

That's when the explosion happened.

An enormous *boom* that echoed off the buildings and distant mountains, ringing in their ears as amusement vanished and they both shot to their feet.

A billowing cloud of smoke rose over the roof of Timberwolf Lodge.

~

New York Times Bestselling Author Vivian Arend
brings you a light-hearted paranormal trilogy
Timberwolf Lodge.

WIN A WILDERNESS LODGE!

Ready for the chance of a lifetime? Enter now to become
the new owners of the Timberwolf Lodge located near
Jasper, Alberta. You'll have one year to meet the set
conditions and the lodge will be all yours!

Small print: (very, very, very small print)
Warning: Lodge may contain werewolves, fated mates, and
tons of shifter pack drama.
Good luck, and have fun! Don't die!

~

Timberwolf Lodge
The Alpha Option
The Enforcer's Gamble
The Omega's Prize

~

ABOUT THE AUTHOR

New York Times and *USA Today* bestselling author Vivian Arend loves to share the products of her over-active imagination with her readers. She writes contemporary, western, and light-hearted paranormal romances. The stories are humorous yet emotional, usually with a large cast of family or friends, and a guaranteed happily-ever-after. Vivian lives in British Columbia, Canada, with her husband of many years—her inspiration for every hero and a willing companion for all sorts of adventures.

www.vivianarend.com